Billionaire Surfer

MISHA BELL

♠ MOZAIKA PUBLICATIONS ♠

Published by Mozaika Publications, an imprint of Mozaika LLC.
www.mozaikallc.com

Cover by Najla Qamber Designs
www.najlaqamberdesigns.com

ISBN: 978-1-63142-858-6
Paperback ISBN: 978-1-63142-861-6

"You got me a vacation?" I gape at my friends.

I knew they'd cover this brunch, which is why I chose a modestly priced place, but a trip to Florida? Seriously?

"You see that?" Jolene says with her signature grin, one that makes her look like the love child of the Joker and the demon clown from *It*... but gorgeous. If she were a dog, she'd be an Australian Shepherd, which is a majestic creature that, to my dismay, rarely requires a haircut. "She almost did a spit take there," she continues.

As always, Dorothy shakes her head disapprovingly at Jolene's antics. Her spirit dog would be a sad-eyed Basset Hound—another breed that, unfortunately, goes hair-cut-less.

These two do not consider themselves friends with each other, only with me, which makes it all the more mind-boggling that they would team up to do anything, especially something as logistically advanced as planning me a last-minute vacay.

Dorothy turns her attention to me. "You need it," she states firmly.

"Brooklyn needs *it* bad," Jolene says. "So bad, in fact, that I finally found something I agree on with Grandma here."

Yep. Dorothy is a cat person while Jolene is a dog person, so they get along about as well as their pets would. Then again, some cats get along well with dogs, so bad analogy.

Dorothy narrows her eyes. "I'm the youngest at this table."

Strictly speaking, that is true. We met when we were freshmen at Brooklyn College—insert jokes about my name here. Having graduated high school a year early, Dorothy was sixteen, and I was seventeen to Jolene's eighteen. Of course, unlike me, my friends graduated and got nice-paying jobs that allow them to make grand gestures such as this trip.

"You're only biologically younger," Jolene says.

"How else can you be younger?" Dorothy demands.

"In spirit," Jolene says. "Yours is that of a seventy-year-old virgin with a dried-up—"

"Hush," I grit out in the tone I usually reserve for calming my first-grader son and his buddies. "I can't accept this."

"Told you," Jolene says to Dorothy and takes a dainty sip from her mimosa glass. To me, she says, "It's all nonrefundable, and neither of us can use it."

My jaw ticks. "I can't go. I have a job—"

"I spoke to one of the other groomers," Dorothy says. "Neveah, I think her name was. She said she'd cover for you."

"Neveah?" I sigh. "My clients will be pissed. That woman makes every dog look like a poodle."

"I can ask someone else." Dorothy's voice turns steely. "But you're going, and that's final."

"What about Reagan?" I demand. "Which one of you is going to babysit?"

That is not to say I'd *let* them babysit. If he stays with Jolene, he'll end up with a girlfriend that he'll get pregnant in short order. And I'm not saying that Reagan himself was a byproduct of her influence on *me*... but it was she who dragged me to the bar where I met the sperm donor who knocked me up. Not that things would be better if he were to stay with Dorothy. He might end up with the opposite fate—though I'm not sure what that is. Joining the clergy? Wearing sandals with socks?

Jolene shudders. "We're not saints. Well, I'm not. We've got him covered, though. There's a sleepaway camp near your Airbnb—also all paid for and nonrefundable."

"A camp?" I look at Dorothy.

"Reputable," Dorothy says. "Zero fatalities so far."

"Zero fatalities. Great."

"You know how social he is," Jolene chimes in. "He'll have a blast, and you know it."

The truth of her statement just makes me feel guilty

about not being able to afford him a trip to a summer camp myself.

My shoulders stoop. "Why would you do this?"

"Because you just turned twenty-five," Jolene says. "That's a round number."

"Round numbers have a zero at the end," Dorothy counters.

"Twenty-five is rounder than twenty-four or twenty-six," Jolene replies smugly.

"That's not the 'why' I meant," I say. "Why cover a vacation and not, say, a month of my rent?" The latter would probably help me more in the grand scheme of things—not that I'd take their money.

"You desperately need vitamin D," Jolene says, waggling her perfectly groomed blond eyebrows.

I nearly choke on my mimosa. In Jolene parlance, the D stands for "dick," which is why I expect Dorothy to cringe, but she nods instead.

"Is that why you pushed for Florida?" she asks Jolene. Turning to me, she adds, "You *are* looking pale. Has your doctor said you're deficient?" The unstated "If so, why didn't you tell me immediately?" is loud and clear.

The evil smile on Jolene's face is out of control. "I'm sure Brooklyn's doctor would say she needs that D. Bad."

Dorothy's already-worried expression grows even more concerned. "Vitamin D is critical for your bones."

"Yeah," Jolene says to me meaningfully. "When was the last time you even thought about... a bone?"

Dorothy squints at the toilet-white skin of my face.

"If the deficiency is bad, maybe you should consider some supplements?"

Is Jolene about to make a dildo joke?

"Yeah, take that D *orally*," Jolene says. "Great idea."

Dorothy frowns. "Orally? As opposed to what, skin patches? I don't think those work."

Jolene grins wider. "I, personally, prefer to take the D as a vaginal suppository, but on occasion, taking it rectally can—"

"How do you always manage to steer every conversation toward genitals?" Dorothy demands from Jolene. Turning to me, she adds, "Mushrooms have vitamin D. Salmon too, and—"

"It's just too much." I push the tickets away. "I gave the two of you papier-mâché figurines for your birthdays."

"I love my Wonder Woman," Dorothy says.

I sigh. "It's actually the Statue of Liberty."

"And I love Mr. Big Cock," Jolene says.

I purse my lips. "I told you many times... it's the Leaning Tower of Pisa."

"Point is, you deserve a break," Dorothy says. "And you forget how you helped me with my grandmother when she was sick."

"And me when Mr. Goobers was having that issue with his penis."

"All I did was help him retract his lipstick," I say with an eyeroll. "Hair getting stuck there is a common problem for fluffy dogs. And your grandmother,

Dorothy, is the sweetest lady I've ever known. It was my pleasure to help her."

Jolene waggles her eyebrows again. "Was it a pleasure to help Mr. Goobers?"

"Eww, stop it," Dorothy says, wrinkling her nose. "I thought bestiality was where even you drew the line, but I guess I was mistaken."

"Seriously, though," I say. "I cannot accept this."

"Then I guess both the camp and the Airbnb will go to waste," Jolene says, sighing dramatically. "And the next time you offer to give Mr. Goobers a free haircut, I'll have no choice but to refuse. And I'll get a vet to help with his penis too."

Grr. She's got me there. Not with the Mr. Goobers haircuts and penis bits, obviously. It's the nonrefundable status of their extremely expensive gift that makes it pretty much impossible to refuse.

"I need to talk to my son," I say, grasping at straws. "If he refuses to go—"

"Reagan? You're kidding me, right? He'll be jumping higher than Mr. Goobers for treats," Jolene says. "But do whatever you need to feel comfortable. Because you're going on this vacation, and you're getting that D deficiency fixed."

———

"Summer camp!?" Reagan shouts before I can tell him any details, such as that there will be no cannibals there. "Thank you, thank you, thank you!" He starts running around the house like one of my four-legged clients when they get the zoomies.

Jolene was right. He's clearly over the moon. So much so my chest squeezes unpleasantly. I'll need to figure out how to give him more experiences like this.

But also... would it hurt my son to at least pretend he'll miss the person who was in labor trying to give birth to him for thirty-five torturous hours?

———

On the flight to Jacksonville, Reagan plays his video game while I do my best not to snap at him or any other innocent bystanders. Thanks to my shit luck, the Red Wedding arrived mere hours ago, giving me the kind of cramps that, if you gave them to a prisoner of war, would go against the Geneva Conventions.

Thanks, body. Was a relaxing plane ride too much to ask for?

I glare at my wrist where my birthday gift from last year resides. It's an Octothorpe Glorp, a fitness tracker that's supposed to warn me when Aunt Flo is coming to town. Often, I imagine the gizmo talking back to me in a voice that's a mix of Richard Simmons and Gollum:

My dear Precious, if I could, I'd keep every tampon you've ever used in a shrine and glue to them the smiles I cut out of my favorite pictures of you. Alas, when it comes to the feature you mention, I merely track your cycles, not predict them.

I suffer the rest of the flight as stoically as I can. Once

we land, I rent a car and drive Reagan straight to the camp—a beachy and chill establishment that plays Jimmy Buffett on a loop.

"Okay, bye," Reagan says without a second of hesitation before running off to check the place out.

I wait to make sure he doesn't run back and tell me he doesn't like what he sees. Nope. He probably thinks I've already left, or has forgotten that I exist altogether.

"He'll have access to a phone," the nearest Boy-Scout-looking counselor says to me reassuringly. "And we have your number on file. Once he's settled in, he'll give you a call. Go."

With a sigh, I head back to the car and start driving.

My mood was already crummy, but now it's worse than that of a stressed-out, sleep-deprived, and tick-riddled hippopotamus. The green and idyllic nature around me only makes me feel shitty about where I actually live, as do the much nicer roads and cleaner streets. But then I almost run over an-honest-to-goodness live alligator and feel a little better about the comparison between my namesake in NYC and Palm Islet, Florida, the illustrious little town where my vacation is to be. Same goes when a deer tries to commit suicide by car a few minutes later, and when the woman in the car in front of me stops to rescue a turtle—getting peed on in the process.

Got to love Florida.

My Airbnb turns out to be located in a gated community, and the female security guard at the entrance is as thorough as a TSA officer. When all my papers seem to be in order, she wrinkles her nose and mutters something about the HOA usually prohibiting Airbnb rentals in the community, and that mine is a rare exception to the rule. She further informs me that the HOA usually charges an overnight guest fee, but that the owner of *my* Airbnb is exempt from "all the rules."

Oh, the humanity. How do the poor members of the HOA sleep at night? As I drive away, it takes effort not to ask if the HOA in this case stands for Hilariously Overbearing Authority.

Driving through the community, I notice that the houses are charming mixes of Spanish, Mediterranean, and Caribbean styles, and that they all have impeccable lawns—must be the same HOA ruling with an iron fist. But when I pull into the cul-de-sac where my Airbnb is located, the monotone pattern is broken. Houses number four and five on Gatorview Drive are twins, and both have sharp corners, are covered in mirrored surfaces and tons of chrome, and remind me of something you might see in a modern art museum.

Since one of these is mine, I assume both belong to the same HOA rules-exempt owner.

My mood lifts minutely as I spot the lake adjacent to both houses, with untouched nature on the opposite bank. The view from my Airbnb must be spectacular, though slightly less so than from the neighboring house.

I check my fitness tracker for the time.

Dearest Precious ought to consider taking more steps, to

tighten those succulent thighs for my stalking—I mean viewing—pleasure.

Crap. I'm too early for check in, and it's getting pretty hot. According to Evan, who's been sending me taciturn texts on behalf of this Airbnb, the code for the garage lock can only be used after eleven-thirty, but I may die of heatstroke by then.

Also, I kind of want the vacation to start, along with the associated relaxation.

Why don't I test said code now?

Walking up to the garage, I type in the code and the door opens. Score! Between this and the lack of a car in the driveway or in the garage, I'm pretty sure I can get inside the house.

After parking in the garage, I open the door to the house proper—which, according to Evan, is the entrance I'll use to come and go.

The door leads right into an ultra-modern kitchen the size of my whole apartment, and there, on the granite island, stands a spread of yummy tapas.

Now this is a fancy welcome. I spot a tiny piece of grilled salmon, a giant bean, a side of rice, an assortment of pickles, a ton of tiny vegetable plates, and something that looks and smells just like miso soup.

Japanese tapas?

Shrugging, I taste the salmon as I take in the lake view through a floor-to-ceiling window.

I'm jealous of Floridians yet again. In New York, you'd have to be a billionaire to have anything close to this house with this kind of view.

The fish is divine, so I sample each of the veggies, which are also amazing. Even the bean is tasty, and the miso soup is the best of its kind, sweet and savory in equal measure.

Suddenly, I hear rustling on the other side of the island.

What the hell?

The island is blocking my view, so I gingerly step over to where the sound is coming from—a sink that I couldn't see earlier.

I gasp.

A man is getting to his feet. Based on the tools scattered on the floor, I assume he must be a plumber here to fix said sink.

Now I'll admit, until today, if I were forced to picture a plumber in my head, he (is that sexist?) would look like Super Mario with a cartoonish mustache, coveralls, and as much sex appeal as a blobfish.

This plumber, however, has to be the hottest man I've ever seen.

His eyes are the clear blue of a Siberian Husky, his hair is the sun-bleached shade of a Golden Retriever's coat, and his sharp angular facial features are godlike with no dog analogs. Sadly, his ears are covered by headphones, but I bet they are sexy too. Oh, and his bare chest boasts an army of glistening muscles that include a six pack. Also, his nipples are hard.

Correction, it's *my* nipples that are hard.

Spotting me, he frowns, but he makes even grumpy

look good. Then his gaze falls on what remains of the tapas, and his eyes beam icicles at me.

"Who are you?" he demands in a low growl that somehow manages to be sexy. "And why did you eat my fucking breakfast?"

Chapter Two

EVAN

Twenty minutes earlier

I'm starving. If I don't eat soon, I think I might pass out.

Fasting cardio is the stupidest idea since wrestling alligators and hunting eagles using drones.

After my morning jog on the beach, I'm like a bear who's woken up after a long winter, and I'm talking typical bears, not the garbage-rummaging troublemakers we have around these parts that don't even need to hibernate on account of the warm weather. I have a headache, zero energy, and feel extremely irate (like said bear), especially about the stupidities of the world, of which there are many. Case in point: I was about to eat my breakfast after examining the house for the next renter, but I've just discovered that the sink is clogged after going over to wash my hands.

Can someone remind me why I do this? I thought it

was because I like to socialize with people from different places, but now I'm starting to suspect that I have a masochistic streak.

What I didn't anticipate is that besides the socializing, you also learn what kind of things people stick in the garbage disposal unit. Thus far, I've seen a blond wig, a deer's horn, a bike tire, and enough dildos and butt plugs to stock a sex-toy shop.

Fucker. I have to see what it is. I won't be able to enjoy my meal until I have this taken care of. Maybe I'll start my own trend—fasting plumbing.

Taking off my shirt, I get under the sink and add a new clog-causer to my collection: a plush Pokémon, specifically Pikachu.

My first instinct is to write the family a bad review on Airbnb and charge them a fee, but I quickly change my mind. I hate bad reviews with a passion, so the Golden Rule says I shouldn't dish them out unless I really mean it, and at the moment, it could be my hanger tempting me.

What I need is a meal, followed by some cuddles with Harry and Sally. If I'm still pissed about Pikachu tomorrow, I'll write the review then. Though I already know I won't because I've never written bad reviews about other guests whose miscellaneous items have clogged the same disposal unit.

Climbing out from under the sink, I hear something, which makes my starved-for-nourishment heart jump.

An intruder?

Unlikely in a gated community, but not impossible.

I carefully rise to my feet.

It's a woman.

A tall, slender woman with shiny hair the color of chocolate, eyes the most delicious shade of caramel, vanilla-ice-cream skin, and a mouth as ripe as—

Fuck. I need to eat so I can stop seeing the whole world in food terms.

Then my eyes fall on my breakfast, the thing I've been fantasizing about.

It's gone.

This *thief* ate it.

No.

Fuck, no.

"Who are you?" I jerk the headphones off my ears. "And why did you eat my fucking breakfast?"

The stranger's hands go to her hips. "I'm renting this place. Who are *you*?"

So, this is Brooklyn... from Brooklyn. "You're *not* renting anything yet," I grit out. "Last I checked, New York and Palm Islet are in the same time zone, and it's not yet eleven-thirty in either place."

She takes a step back, but then her eyes go slitty. "So... *this* is what passes for customer service around here?"

My jaw ticks. "Let me reiterate. You're not a customer. Not yet. You're more like a trespasser, and around these parts, they often get shot."

"Ah, so you're full-on psycho?" She scans me without the fear that should come along with her statement. As her gaze lands on my hand, her eyes widen. "Is that a ripped-up stuffed animal?"

Shit. I've been clutching the late Pikachu like a stress ball. Maybe I do look like a psycho... or worse, like the stereotype of a native Floridian.

I open the trash and bury Pikachu's remains there without a eulogy. "The little brat who left this morning stuffed that toy into the garbage disposal."

Brooklyn lifts her pointed little chin. "So not only are you rude, you also hate children."

Hate children? My hackles rise higher. I've heard that accusation before—granted, under different circumstances—and it's as untrue as it is infuriating.

"What else?" she continues. "Do you punch old ladies in your spare time?"

Are these hypothetical old ladies part of the HOA? Either way, I'd never punch one... no matter how tempting those particular ladies sometimes make the proposition.

"I'm rude?" I gesture at my would-be meal. "*I* didn't sneak in and eat *your* food."

"Can't you let that go already?" She plants her feet wider, like a boxer ready to go another round. "I thought the tapas were here as a warm welcome. Clearly, you don't know the meaning of the term."

"Tapas?" I wipe a bead of sweat off my brow. "That was a traditional Japanese breakfast."

She wrinkles her nose. "Salmon for breakfast?"

I blow out a frustrated breath. "Now you're dissing a whole culture?"

"No," she says. "Just you."

"Don't New Yorkers put lox on their bagels?" I say. "That's salmon too."

She scoffs. "Doesn't everyone put lox on their bagels?"

Touché. Also, thinking of a bagel with lox makes my stomach rumble so loudly that she does a double take. Then, for the first time, something resembling guilt appears on her face.

"Look," she says. "Obviously, if I had known it was your food, I wouldn't have eaten it."

I take a breath and force my bunched shoulders down. "Is that an apology?"

She visibly bristles. "Are you going to apologize for being a dick?"

"No, but you might as well consider yourself checked in early."

There.

I feel like a saint as I stomp out of the kitchen, at least until I smell her perfume or whatever it is. Yuzu, sage, and cloves. Delicious.

Fuck me. My stomach is at it again.

Slamming the door behind me, I hurry to my own place—where a much crappier breakfast awaits.

Chapter Three

BROOKLYN

As the asshole passes by me, my nose detects starfruit, ocean salt, and wax. Hmm. When combined with the way he looks, the last two scents make me think he might be a surfer in his spare time.

But aren't surfers more chill? His personality is what most people think pit bulls are like, and Chihuahuas—though those unfair dog stereotypes are breedist.

"Wait, you forgot your tools!" I shout, but he doesn't hear me.

Great. This means I'll probably have to see him again.

I drag in a calming breath and finish the last of his breakfast, since I might as well. When the food is gone, I swallow my last Advil and walk out onto the screened porch to examine the giant pool facing the lake.

Wow.

Even if I weren't minutes away from the beach, this vacation would still be amazing.

Maybe I can actually relax for the first time in seven years?

I plop on a nearby chaise, but instead of relaxing, my mind starts replaying the interaction with the hot plumber, and I wonder if I overreacted. Maybe some period-induced irritability?

Oh, well. At least I have my hormones as an excuse. What is his?

Suddenly, an annoying noise reaches my ears. It's a loud buzzing that reminds me of a giant vacuum cleaner from hell.

Speaking of hell, why am I smelling sulfur?

I scan my surroundings. There's a sprinkler running on the right side of the lawn, but those aren't *that* loud.

Then I see where the noise is coming from. The plumber is riding some hellish machine over the grass, still shirtless.

He's either cutting the grass or filming an ad for said machine—and I suddenly feel like buying one.

I guess he's more than just a plumber.

"Hey!" I shout.

No reaction.

"Dude!"

Nope. He's got headphones on, so between that and the noise, I doubt he can hear himself think... assuming he ever engages in that activity.

I open the door of the porch screen and wave my arms.

He finally stops the racket and takes his headphones off.

"Can you *not* do that?" I shout.

His eyes narrow. "Not do what? Exist?"

I roll my eyes. "You can exist all you want, but maybe without so much noise?"

"Oh." He looks down at his mount. "Is the grass cutting bothering you?"

Was that sarcasm? "Yes! It would bother anyone with ears. Any chance you can do it some other time?"

He sighs. "The original plan was to do this *before* you checked in, but we know how *that* turned out."

I match his sigh. "So... is that a 'no?'"

He blows out an annoyed breath. "When would it be more convenient for you, Your Majesty?"

"Does it always sound like that?" I ask.

He gives me an irritated bob of the head.

I look at the perfectly reasonable height of the grass. "Can you do it *after* I leave?" A time he most likely awaits with great anticipation.

The guy scans the grass like he's never seen it before. "If I don't do it soon, someone from the HOA will moan, and they're much more annoying than you."

Is that a veiled compliment or an indictment of the HOA?

"Maybe you could do it while I'm away," I suggest.

He wipes a few beads of sweat off his torso in an extremely distracting way. "And when will that be?"

I banish sweat-licking fantasies from my mind. "I'll need to go get groceries soon." Including more Advil, because my headache is just getting worse and worse, though my cramps have eased up somewhat. My uterus seems to be happier at the moment. No idea why.

"When is soon?"

"An hour?" I set a timer on my phone.

"Fine," he says.

"Great. Now... do you know what that awful smell is?"

He sniffs the air before a hint of a smile touches his eyes. "The one reminiscent of rotten eggs?"

I nod.

"The sprinklers here use well water," he says. "This is what it smells like."

As if to confirm his words, wind blows in my direction from the sprinkler and tests my gagging reflex.

"Any chance you can run the sprinklers some other time?" I ask.

Do I sound entitled? If so, I blame him for that too—in that, he brings out the worst in me.

He curls his upper lip. "If it will suit Your Majesty, I'll run the sprinklers before sunrise."

"Great. Thanks."

"Will that be all?" he asks, all but daring me to tack on something else.

"You forgot your tools on the kitchen floor," I say.

"I'll get them in an hour," he says, then restarts the abominable machine and rides away, leaving gasoline fumes in his wake.

I head back inside and sit on a comfy couch that has a view of the stinky sprinklers. I'm not going back outside until I see the water go away.

As I sit, I feel some obscene pang of disappointment at the sight of the tools he left behind. Does a part of me *want* him to stop by to get them when I *am* home? If so, what is wrong with that part of me? Has Jolene somehow gotten into my head?

No, I'm not being fair to Jolene. When she preached about me needing some D, this isn't what she meant. Even she knows the difference between getting some dick and getting together with a dick.

Not that I'd go for the former on this vacation either, regardless of how nice the guy attached to it may be. That one casual hookup that forever changed my life was my last. If I have sex, it will have to be as part of a real relationship, and that will not happen on a vacation. The most I could hope for in such a distant zip code is a fling, which is basically an extended hookup.

Either way, even if the plumber/grasscutter were a New Yorker, he wouldn't be relationship material.

My phone rings.

It's Reagan. He gushes about how much he loves the camp for a few minutes before he asks how things are going with me.

"Great, kiddo," I say. "The place is very nice. I'm going to shop for groceries and maybe check out the beach after that."

"We're going to the beach later today," he says excitedly, and he tells me the whole itinerary that precedes the beach trip before launching into a story about the friends he's already made.

Speaking of friends, I start a conference call with

mine as soon as I hang up to thank them again for the incredible gift.

"Send pictures of everything," Dorothy demands.

"But maybe not the D," Jolene chimes in. "At least, don't send them to Mrs. Prude."

The sprinklers turn off outside.

So he has come through on that. Good. The least he can do.

I say goodbye to my friends and step outside to lounge by the pool.

When I sit down, I feel a pleasant warm breeze on my skin, and the air is clear of sulfur. All I smell is freshly cut grass.

The pill I took earlier must be kicking in too because I feel semi-normal and on the verge of calm.

Which is probably why the alarm I set earlier goes off at that exact moment.

Right. I promised not to be here when he comes to take his tools and finish grass cutting.

Grr. I get to my feet and check the pool temperature.

Warm and perfect, of course. Another reason why I don't want to leave.

Maybe I don't have to? Maybe I could stick earplugs in and swim while he makes the noise?

No. I think this may be that crazy part of me scheming to have the plumber see me in my bikini—as payback for his tendency to strut around shirtless. Though pale, I'm in pretty good shape, and I haven't had the chance to flaunt that fact in years.

Fine. I'll use the pool later. The ocean might be nicer anyway.

Heading back, I put on my bikini, throw on a summer dress over that, and drive to the local supermarket, where I get only Advil for now—the produce might die if I leave it in the trunk in this heat.

When I step onto the beach, I feel almost giddy. There's something special about the feeling of warm sand between your toes, the sound of the surf, and the view of the endless blue expanse. Something that clears my headache better than any drug.

Also lifting my mood is a very strange sight: a pair of people sitting on the beach on an honest-to-goodness couch. He looks like a Bedlington Terrier, and she like a Chinese Crested Dog.

Why the couch? How? Who cares? I hope what happened was: someone threw the couch away, and this enterprising couple picked it up and decided it would make a great beach chair. Or they've retired their own couch in this way. Hell, for all I know, this might be a Florida tradition, like New Yorkers tying the laces of their old sneakers together and tossing them up to hang from power lines.

With a smile on my face, I walk up to feel the ocean temperature.

It's warm, but there's a big problem if I want to swim: the waves are way overzealous. Also, now that I'm paying attention, I see a red flag nearby and a sign below it that says, "Swimming not recommended today. No lifeguard on duty."

Oh, well. Soaking in the rays might be all the relaxation I need.

Spreading my towel, I sprawl on it, close my eyes, and pretend that I am also sitting on a couch... which is when I drift off to sleep.

———

Why is my mouth so crunchy, why am I so hot, and what is that smell?

I open my eyes and find myself face down in the sand, with the towel covering me like a blanket, instead of staying under me as a loyal beach towel should.

Crap. I have enough sand in my mouth to make a small castle.

Feeling very ladylike, I spend the next few minutes vigorously spitting. Next, I look for some source of water so I can rinse my mouth and figure out the source of the weird smell. If it's well water again, I might just use it to rinse out my mouth, smell or not.

Nope. It's not sprinklers, but something weirder. A cow is standing nearby, and the smell is coming from a patty it's made. And yes, I do mean a regular cow, the type that goes "moo," not a sea cow, as in a manatee, an animal this area is actually famous for. Thanks to the coloring and the sad eyes, she looks just like a giant Basset Hound, only without the droopy ears, and with horns.

I rub my eyes, which is a mistake because now they also feel sandy. Could the cow be a hallucination brought on by heatstroke?

But then why is the couple on that couch looking at her too? I saw *them* before I fell asleep.

More importantly, could the cow give me some milk for a mouth rinse?

I cringe as the scene plays out in front of my eyes: I walk up to the cow, grab her udder—which is basically a boob—and jerk it into my mouth.

Yeah. No, thanks. Maybe if I had stayed in school and become a veterinarian like I'd always wanted, I'd have experience with cows and would be able to do something like that, but not with my pet groomer accolades. The cow would kick me in the head—and be right in doing so —and then I would die and become one of those "only in Florida" stories on the news.

Belatedly, I recall the bathroom I saw near where I parked, so that is where I go to rinse my mouth.

Except a sign over the sink says, "Danger. Non-potable water, do not drink."

Hmm. Clearly, you're allowed to wash your hands with this water, so the big question is: would rinsing my mouth be closer to drinking or handwashing?

Fuck it. I cup some water and rinse my mouth, then my eyes.

Ah. So much better. Hopefully, I didn't just get pink eye and cholera.

I return to my towel just in time to witness a mustachioed Bull Terrier-looking dude depositing the cow poop into a big bag, the way dog owners do for their charges.

Weird. The Bull Terrier then leads the cow away—

before anyone gets the chance to ask any obvious questions.

My theory is that it was one of those Kobe beef cows —no relation to the famous basketball player. Allegedly, those cows are treated like royalty, receiving beer, massages, and probably pedicures too. If any of that is true, why not throw in a stroll on the beach?

Pondering this question some more, I sit on my towel and admire the wavy ocean.

Hmm. Despite the no-swim sign, there are surfers in the distance.

In fact, one of them even has a Golden Retriever on the surfboard with him. How cute is that?

I sigh wistfully. Reagan would have a blast if he saw this. He loves videos of dogs doing all sorts of fun things, from singing to typing. He'd also make a good argument for going for a swim... and not being a chicken.

Maybe I'll just walk in until the water is up to my knees. That way, I can get my face wet and cool off a little. Surely that should be safe.

Gingerly, I approach the water and wade in until my ankles are wet—which is when a huge wave comes out of nowhere.

Whoosh!

My world spins as I'm knocked off my feet.

I flail my arms as water surrounds me on all sides, but it's to no avail. The water drags me back into the ocean, and my life plays before my eyes as I prepare to drown.

Chapter Four

EVAN

A few hours earlier

As soon as I feel full from my boring cereal bowl, I realize that I acted sub-optimally when I met the new renter. She assumed my food was a welcome spread waiting for her—not *that* crazy of an assumption. I've actually toyed with the idea of leaving snacks out, but I've never implemented it.

I blow out a breath. In my defense, she didn't need to be so truculent. Still, I will strongly consider apologizing if I get the chance.

Except when I start cutting the grass, there she is, even more adversarial than before.

Fuck. Why is it always the attractive ones? Forget the apology. I'll just avoid her for the duration of her stay, which kind of sucks since we're next door to each other, and she's the only person younger than sixty-five in a ten-mile radius.

Whatever. Since I have the energy and the lawn-mower, I cut the grass for one of my nicer, elderly neighbors—one of the few who don't give me HOA-related grief.

When the hour is up, I make sure Brooklyn's car is not in the garage, then cut the rental's lawn. Afterward, I walk in to get my tools from the kitchen—and there she is.

Sally, my cat.

"How are you here?" I ask.

She slowly blinks at me, and it's not difficult to guess what that lazy gaze is saying:

Well, duh. Using our wiles, we escaped the evil palace where our captor hides us away from the tomcat-in-shining-armor.

With a sigh, I grab Sally and the tools before heading home, where I find one of the sliding doors slightly ajar, which is probably how she got out.

"How did you open that?" I demand.

Sally swishes her tail.

Wiles, remember?

Harry, my dog, runs up to me and wags his tail with so much enthusiasm you'd think I was gone for a year.

Human dude and cat dudette. You're both finally home. Awesome sauce.

I fill both of their food bowls, and while they eat, I get everything ready for a trip to the beach.

As soon as Harry is done with his food, he sprints over to sniff the surfboard.

Don't forget me, bro. You know how much I like to ride them waves.

I smile. "I'm going more for you than for me, so you're coming, don't worry."

I load Harry and the board into the car. As I grab my keys, Sally gives me a baleful glare.

If our evil captor so much as hints about bringing us near that obscene amount of water, eyes will be gouged.

———

Everything is as usual on the beach: Boone and Bonnie are sitting on the couch they found at a junkyard a week ago, and in the far distance, Calvin is walking one of his pet cows.

No. Wait. Something is different. There's a woman lying on the sand.

Given how pale her back is, she's either a tourist or a vampire.

Just my luck. The locals don't mind when Harry is off leash, but she might.

As I get closer, I recognize her. It's Brooklyn, and she's not sunbathing. At least not on purpose. She seems to have fallen asleep face down in the sand, and has somehow rolled away from her towel too.

It's a good thing the house she rented has a king-sized bed, or else she'd probably fall off.

I wince as I watch the sun mercilessly bake her smooth, pretty skin. Even if she's wearing sunblock, she'll have second-degree burns in an hour.

The humane thing to do would be to wake her, but then she'd bite my head off.

No, I need another idea. If I had an umbrella in the car, I'd set it up here, but I don't. So, risking my balls and sanity, I pick up her towel and cover her with it to prevent further sun exposure.

There. I doubt she'd do something like that for me.

Harry looks at the ocean and whines.

"Yeah, yeah," I tell him. "We're going."

Once Harry is dressed in his canine flotation device, I take my board and we wade into the waves.

Ahh. Only surfing brings me this intense feeling of relaxation mixed with exhilaration, peace with terror, and above all, an almost spiritual sense of freedom. Harry loves it too and has such a blast that he makes me appreciate surfing all the more. I'm also grateful that he's in my life because he often drags me to do this when I need it the most.

Just as I'm riding a big kahuna, I see Brooklyn approach the water and all my joy evaporates.

Can't the woman read? The sign says very plainly that the ocean isn't safe. Even Harry and I have to be careful today, and we've been coming to this beach our whole lives—not to mention, he has water-rescue training and I'm a certified lifeguard.

"Don't!" I shout, but I doubt she can hear me over the surf.

Damn it. She's stepping into the water. Doesn't she see—

Fuck.

The wave that was clearly headed her way knocks her off her feet.

"Help her," I command Harry and point at her before I leap into action, a burst of adrenaline propelling me toward the shore.

I beat Harry to the scene, but I don't see Brooklyn on the surface, and when I dive, it's all muddy sand.

A moment later, Harry barks, his nose pointing to a spot a couple of feet away.

Heart hammering in my chest, I dive there—and there she is.

As quickly as I can, I position my surfboard under her chest to keep her head above water. Moving faster than I thought possible, I get her onto dry sand, then move her so she is splayed on the surfboard, safely away from any waves that might come.

"I'm calling 911!" Bonnie yells from the couch.

I don't thank Bonnie now, but I will later—at this point, every millisecond counts.

I check to see if Brooklyn's breathing.

Nothing.

Even as ice spreads through my veins, my training kicks in, and I begin CPR.

At first, there's no effect.

As I inhale in preparation for another rescue breath, she gasps, then rolls over and vomits ocean water, her eyes wild and scared.

I hold her hair and soothingly stroke her back. As her spasms ease, I help her lie back on the board. She closes her eyes, still breathing raggedly. As I watch her chest move, it feels like I'm relearning to breathe too. I don't know why I got as tense as I did, probably because this is my first real rescue attempt.

A few seconds later, Brooklyn opens her eyes, looking a bit calmer. She may be okay, but I don't let myself relax. Looks can be deceiving.

"The wave came," she says haltingly.

"It did." I'm proud of how soothing I sound given my overwhelming temptation to chastise her for walking into such a tumultuous ocean.

"Did I almost drown?" she asks.

I nod, ice filling my stomach anew at the knowledge of how close she came to dying. "But you're breathing now, and the paramedics are on their way," I say, to reassure myself as much as her. "You should be all right."

She sits up. "Paramedics? No. I don't need that. I'm already all right."

"You almost drowned." Maintaining a soothing tone is becoming more difficult. "You need to go to the hospital."

She wrinkles her nose. "I don't like hospitals."

My jaw ticks. "Only hypochondriacs *like* hospitals. And maybe not even them."

"But I'm breathing fine," she says stubbornly.

"You're going to the hospital," I grit out.

She narrows her eyes. "You can't tell me what to do."

I sigh in exasperation. "I'm obviously not going to drag you to the damn hospital. Neither will the paramedics. But you could have organ damage from the lack of oxygen, so you *should* go."

She blinks. "All I wanted was to just relax, for the first time in forever," she says, her voice cracking—like she's on the verge of tears. "Is that too much to ask?"

I liked it much more when she was angry and irritable. This vulnerable side of her twists something in my gut. "Look, Brooklyn," I say gently. "If the doctors clear you, you'll still have six more days to relax. And the rest of today."

"I think I've forgotten how to relax," she says.

"In that case, I'll help you," I shock myself by saying. "I'll take you to a beach without waves. And then Sealand—a nearby seaquarium run by a guy I went to high school with. And if you like that one, we can also go to Octoworld, a place where—"

The siren of the ambulance drowns out my next words.

When the cacophony eases, Brooklyn sighs. "Fine. I'll go to the stupid hospital."

"*We'll* go," I say. "I'm coming with you."

"You are?" she asks, looking at the paramedics fearfully.

"If that's okay with you," I say.

She catches my gaze. "Thank you. For everything."

I scratch the back of my head. "No problem."

"I'm going to ask a stupid question," she says with a flush. "What's your name?"

Chapter Five

BROOKLYN

I feel like a complete idiot—and not just because of my last question. After all the grief I've given him, the guy has saved my life, yet still I manage to bitch at him.

"I'm Evan." He extends his callused hand to me, and as soon as I shake it, I feel like I'm drowning again—this time in hormones that go haywire from his touch.

Maybe there's something to the notion that when you have a brush with death, you feel like having sex to prove that you're alive. Or maybe Jolene is wiser than anyone has given her credit for. Maybe this strong reaction is due to a severe dick deficiency. Alternatively, it could be that I *do* have oxygen-deprivation-related brain damage.

"And you're Brooklyn," Evan states, dragging me out of my stupor.

"Guilty as charged. I take it you're the Evan I was corresponding with," I say.

Which means he's not only the plumber and grass cutter, but he manages the property as well.

Behind Evan, I spot the paramedics with a stretcher. He follows my gaze, then turns back and says, "It's going to be okay."

The dog that he was surfing with whines. He must realize Evan is planning to go with me in the ambulance and that dogs can't join.

Unless they can?

Evan turns to the couple on the couch. "Boone, Bonnie, can Harry hang with you?"

Upon hearing his name, Harry wags his tail.

Despite the circumstances, I smile. I love animals in general, and dogs and cats in particular. This specific canine is gorgeous too, and his face reminds me of that of his human.

"Sure thing," Bonnie replies with a heavy Southern drawl.

"Thank you," Evan says. "And thanks for calling 911 when you did."

A tooth is missing from Bonnie's otherwise very toothy grin. "Any time, sugar. Any. Time."

Flirting so shamelessly in front of her husband? Then again, maybe Boone is her brother? Or—and this might not be a kind thought—could he be both?

Harry wags his tail at the arriving paramedics, but they ignore him and focus on me.

Out of the corner of my eye, I see Evan put on some clothes.

What a pity. His shirtless torso would've been a welcome distraction on this otherwise unpleasant trip.

After a bumpy ride on the stretcher, I find myself inside the ambulance, a (regrettably) fully dressed Evan at my side.

"Did the EMTs give you any grief?" I ask. "I thought only family was allowed to ride in the back."

For the first time in our acquaintance, Evan smiles, and it's like a sunrise over a calm ocean. "Palm Islet is a relatively small town. I know the EMTs, and who they allow in the back is up to their discretion."

If true, the EMTs in question must find Evan trustworthy.

Hmm. The odd thing is that I'm starting to find him trustworthy as well, and that's unheard of for me. After Reagan's father evaporated from our lives, I stopped trusting the males of my species. Then again, Evan saved my life, and the only other man who's done that was the doctor at Coney Island Hospital seven years ago. I trust him too, though I thankfully haven't needed to see him since.

I clear my throat. "Sorry about earlier. I dislike hospitals and took that out on you."

Evan waves it off. "I hate hospitals myself. If our roles had been reversed, I might've acted the same way."

The deep pain behind those words is evident in the storm in his eyes. It makes me want to rise from the stretcher and give him a huge hug, but instead, I reach out and clasp his big hand in both of mine. "What happened?"

He stares at our joined hands in confusion, then meets my gaze. "How do you know that something happened?"

I bite my lip. "Because I hate hospitals for the same reason. Something bad happened to me there."

His eyebrows snap together. "What was it? Are you okay?"

"I am now." I take a breath and blurt, "I almost died at a hospital. If it weren't for this one surgeon, I wouldn't be here today."

The full story is that I did the aforementioned almost-dying after childbirth, but I don't want to share that part, partly because the details are grisly to men, but also because, for some unfathomable reason, I don't want him to know that I'm a mom.

Wait. What? That last bit is so dumb I want to slap myself. Am I picturing us in a relationship or something? In any case, what's the logic for hiding Reagan? Because Evan so obviously hates kids? But how did I—

"I'm sorry," Evan says softly. "That's a terrible thing to go through." He takes a breath of his own. "My mother was ill for a long time before she passed, and we practically lived in the hospital. Now anytime I drive past it, the memories are..." He trails off.

"Oh, no." Even though I'm estranged from my parents, I can't imagine losing them in such a painful way. I squeeze his hand. "You don't have to go with me. I'll be fine."

"No." He pulls his hand away. "You're not getting rid of me that easily."

I smile weakly. "Okay. If you're sure."

"I'm positive," he says, and in that moment, the ambulance comes to a stop and I'm taken to the ER with Evan at my side.

"Put this on," a nurse demands, handing me a gown.

I go to the changing room and swap my swimsuit and coverup for the gown that makes me feel like a prisoner in Azkaban.

When I come out, the nurse offers to dry my wet clothes—a service that would never happen in NYC.

Once I get my tiny private space, random people in scrubs take my vitals and demand to know what happened.

"Thanks for being here," I say to Evan when there's a second of peace. "I think this would suck much worse if I were alone."

He squeezes my shoulder. "Don't mention it."

His touch skyrockets my pulse so high one of the monitors attached to me beeps. I lean over to check the beeping monitor, but I don't know how to read it, so I glance at my trusty Octothorpe Glorp instead.

Yep. Even now that Evan's hand has been removed, I'm clocking about a hundred-and-twenty beats per minute.

My dear Precious, I'm getting very jealous of all these other gadgets monitoring the majesty that is your body and all its fluids. Know that these others are not as obsessed with you as I am. I don't think any of them watch you sleep every second of every night, and I'm positive none of them fantasize about eating your toenails.

A young, attractive female nurse pops into my space, presumably to check if I'm going into cardiac arrest.

"You're good," she says, and I swear I hear disappointment in her voice.

Hmm. Is it my face?

No. I spot her staring longingly at Evan, which explains it.

"The doctor is on his way," she says to no one in particular and skedaddles.

Whew. I hope I don't have to stay here any longer than necessary, or else she might go Nurse Ratched on my ass.

"The doctor is probably Vic," Evan says with a faint smile. "He's a buddy of mine."

Yep. When the doctor walks in, his tag reads Victor Hugo.

Wait. Isn't that the name of that French author who wrote *Les Misérables* and *The Hunchback of Notre Dame*?

Also, the doc reminds me of the Beauceron dog breed and is nearly as dreamy as Evan. Is there something in the water of Palm Islet?

"Hey, Vic," Evan says. "How's your nana?"

"Better," Vic replies without a hint of a French accent. "She's been gardening, if you can believe that."

"Gardening after a heart attack." Evan shakes his head. "That sounds just like your nana."

Vic—or Dr. Hugo, as I'd rather call him—turns my way. "Let me listen to your lungs."

I sit up, and he does his thing, which makes Evan tense for some reason.

"Okay." Dr. Hugo puts his stethoscope away. "You want the good news first or the bad?"

My feet go cold. "What is it?"

Dr. Hugo shakes his head. "I'm so sorry. I was about to make a bad joke. It's *only* good news. You're free and clear."

"What the fuck?" Evan demands. "Why would you say shit like that?"

"Again, I'm so sorry," Dr. Hugo says to me. "I was going to make a lame joke about the bad news being that you're dating a knucklehead."

"We're not dating." Evan looks on the verge of punching his friend, but then rolls his eyes instead.

Hey, did he need to deny the idea of us dating so vehemently? Obviously, it's absurd, but it's not like Dr. Hugo was out of line for making the assumption, unless Evan thinks that I'm so hideous and bitchy that it *is* out of line...

"Sorry, again," Dr. Hugo says to me. A smile touches his eyes as he adds, "You're healthy and not dating a knucklehead, all great news."

Evan's jaw ticks. "If you ever want to become a comedian, don't quit your day job."

With that, I leap to my feet. "Thanks, Dr. Hugo."

"Please," he says. "Call me Vic."

Was that a death stare Evan just gave him?

Men. With the kind of friends they make, who needs enemies?

"Ready to go?" Evan asks.

I get to my feet and locate the nurse who offered to dry my clothes.

Inside the changing room, I change back and feel almost normal. When I come out, Evan's eyes roam my body. Almost as if—

"You've got a sunburn," Evan says. "A bad one."

So that's it. He doesn't appreciate what he sees—he's horrified.

I crane my neck so I can take a look at my back. All I can see is my shoulder, but it confirms what Evan just said.

It's red. And now that I know, I feel it too.

Shit. I guess with all the adrenaline, I blocked out the burning or thought it was just due to dry skin courtesy of the hospital's air. But there's no mistaking it now. I'm burned, and badly. The last time this happened, I looked like a boiled lobster who dressed up as a beet for Halloween.

"We'd better go," Evan says and leads me outside, where we get a ride back to the beach in the ambulance, thanks to the friendly EMTs.

As soon as we exit the ambulance back at the beach, I feel a burning sensation when the sun touches my exposed skin, particularly on my back.

The sunburn is getting worse.

"Here." Evan covers me in his shirt.

I instantly feel better, but I think that has more to do with his scent on the shirt than the blocked sunrays.

Loud barking in the distance makes us both glance at

Harry, who is having the time of his life chasing a gull by the shore.

"The cow is back," I say, spotting it.

Actually, this must be a slightly different cow. Her coloring reminds me more of a Dalmatian. With eyes more baleful than sad, the cow gives Harry a glare that makes me think of an interesting statistic I read right before this trip: you're five times more likely to be killed by a cow than by a shark.

"Yeah," Evan says in a pretty blasé fashion, considering there's a cow on a beach. "She's one of Calvin's. He has a bunch."

"Why?" I cozy into his shirt and sniff it as surreptitiously as I can.

"You can't just have one cow. They're herd animals," Evan says. "They'd feel lonely, bored, and anxious by themselves."

I grin. "What I meant to ask is, 'Why have cows at all?'"

"Oh." Evan shrugs. "I imagine Calvin got them for the same reason people get cats or dogs from a shelter."

Ah. Right. But still. Cows. Plural. Calvin is either angling for sainthood or is planning to have lots of barbeques when a zombie apocalypse arrives.

On the beach, Harry notices the cow and prances over, tail wagging.

The cow doesn't look happy about this, though it's possible she's just on her period, like me, or is just a grump in general.

"Harry, no!" Evan shouts.

At Evan's voice, Harry's ears perk up, and he sprints over, tail wagging much more excitedly than it did for the cow.

"Ready to head home?" Evan asks me.

I nod, which stretches the skin on my neck and makes it hurt.

Evan frowns. He must've noticed my small wince.

"How about I give you a ride?" he says.

I shake my head. "I have a car here." I wave toward the parking lot.

"Give me your keys," he says. "I'll have Boone bring it to the rental."

I hand over the keys and stay with Harry as Evan makes the arrangements.

"Your human is a lot nicer than I thought," I tell Harry.

Harry wags his tail, which I take for agreement.

"Let's go," Evan says when he returns. He leads me to his ride—a rugged-looking pickup that brings to mind camping and monster-truck fights.

Harry points his nose at the bed of the pickup and whines.

"No, bud." Evan tosses his surfboard where the dog is asking to be. "That's not a safe place to ride."

Turning to me, he explains, "The people who gave him up to the shelter must've let him ride back there, and now he prefers it." He turns to Harry. "I keep telling you: you could fall out, jump out, and let's not even think about what would happen if there was a rear collision."

Huffing stoically, Harry walks over to the door and leaps in when Evan opens it for him.

"One of these days, he'll stop asking," Evan says to me with a grin. "This and beer are his worst vices."

At the mention of beer, Harry's ears perk up.

"No. Beer isn't good for dogs." Evan looks at me. "I had to switch to wine because he'd sometimes steal my beers."

Harry blinks innocently from inside the car.

Smiling, I get in and find the truck cab much roomier than it seemed from the outside. Neither the dog nor his owner is in my way, and I don't have to sit on Evan's lap.

Sigh.

We drive away from the beach and soon stop next to a store with a giant fish statue in the front.

"How do you feel about sashimi?" Evan asks me.

I shrug. "It's tasty, but it's not like I want to eat it every day." Nor could I *afford* to eat it every day. "Why?" Without answering, he runs into the store and comes back out with a bag.

"Seriously," I say when we resume driving. "Why did you ask about sashimi?"

I mean, I have an inkling but—

"As you might've guessed from this morning's breakfast, I'm a fan of Japanese food," Evan says. "So the reason I asked if you like sashimi is because I want to make it for you. Tonight. For dinner."

Chapter Six

EVAN

S hit. How did I manage to make that invite sound so much like a date?

"Oh. Wow," Brooklyn says, no doubt working up to the rejection. "Thanks. I'd love that."

Oh.

Hmm.

She'll come?

Okay. She must not have felt the date-like vibe there.

Good.

I'm not into dating, and especially not dating tourists. Unlike many of my friends, I abhor flings. They remind me of jerking off to porn, but with a higher chance of catching an STD. If I wanted any form of a relationship—and I don't—it would be more along the lines of marriage, but there's a big problem with that. Women don't want to marry me because I will not give them kids. Before I gave up on dating, my relationships would last right up until I revealed my vasectomy. Then the woman would accuse me of hating children—which is not true—and couldn't end things fast enough.

"Doesn't it take great skill to cut sashimi?" Brooklyn asks. "I've seen *Jiro Dreams of Sushi*."

I sit up straighter. "I went to a school in LA. Studied with a sushi sensei and everything."

"Oh?" She regards me curiously. "Are you planning to open a restaurant one day?"

I shake my head. "I just wanted to be able to make it for myself exactly as I like it. And control the freshness too."

"That's a lot of effort," she says. "You *really* like your Japanese food."

I drive into the private entrance of my community, and Brooklyn blinks in confusion.

"Are we eating dinner at my place?" she asks.

"No. I mean, we could, but I have the bamboo board, yanagiba, and everything," I say. "Plus my cat loves sashimi so—"

"You have a cat too?" She sounds oddly jealous.

"Yeah," I say as I pull into my driveway. "She actually escaped to your rental earlier today, and I have no idea why."

"Wait." Brooklyn looks at my house, then at me. "They let you live here?"

"They?"

"The owners of this house and the one I'm staying at. Unless... do they let you stay here as a perk for managing the—"

"I am the owner," I state, figuring her semi-insulting

rant could go on for a month if I let it. "Why would you assume I'm not? Is there something about my clothes or demeanor that screams 'not a homeowner?'"

Brooklyn blushes, and I realize why women invented rouge. On the right face, it's hot.

"I'm sorry," she mutters. "You were fixing the sink, so I figured you were a plumber. Then you were cutting the grass and—"

"I enjoy doing those things myself." I pull the car into my garage and open the door for her. "Usually, when you own real estate, you earn so-called 'passive' income," I say as we walk inside. "That sounds boring, so for me, there's an active component. Until I've built too many houses to manage on my own, I don't plan to hire anyone to help."

"What do you mean by 'too many?'" She gawks around my kitchen—a carbon copy of the one she saw earlier in my other house. "Are you building a lot of houses right now or something?"

"I've just built these two so far, but I own the majority of the land in this community, so eventually, I'll build more."

I don't usually brag about my net worth, but I guess she wounded my pride with her assumption.

Now she gawks at me. "You own the majority of the land here?" Then a lightbulb seems to go off in her brain. "Is that why the guard said something about the HOA rules not applying to you?"

I nod. "I have the majority of the vote at the HOA, so I

treat their silly rules as suggestions only. To put it another way, I let them have their rules." I open the drawer with all my sashimi gear. "If they piss me off, I'll show up to the annoying meetings and vote for the whole community to be run the way I wish. That's why they mostly leave me alone... at least as much as their quarrelsome natures allow."

As I open the bag of fresh fish, Sally materializes as if from thin air and slowly blinks her big eyes at me.

Aha, our wiles strike again. Using mind-fuckery of the highest order, we have successfully manipulated our captor into getting us the sustenance we rightly deserve. Once our belly is full, escape will be imminent.

"Oh, my god," Brooklyn exclaims. "What kind of cat is that?"

"A Ragamuffin." I begin filleting the salmon as Sally looks on so intently you'd think she were either hypnotized or trying to hypnotize me.

We will forgive our captor for the "ragamuffin" insult... this time. But one day, when the tomcat-in-shining-armor saves us, all scores will be settled. In blood.

"You're such a cutie," Brooklyn says to Sally. "What's your name?"

"Sally," I say, in case the cat isn't feeling very chatty at the moment.

"Hold on." Brooklyn drags her gaze away from the cat and examines me with a grin. "Harry and Sally?"

Keeping a poker face, I slice the fish as I've been taught. "What?"

"Oh, please," she says. "*When Harry Met Sally*?"

"He barked," I deadpan. "And she hissed. But now they're best friends. Usually."

Brooklyn groans in irritation. "You know perfectly well that *When Harry Met Sally* is a romantic comedy. With Billy Crystal and Meg Ryan."

I slice the fish some more. "Fine. Yes. That was my mom's favorite movie." The admission simultaneously warms my chest and makes it hurt. I remember Mom and Dad playfully fighting over the last pieces of popcorn when we'd watch that movie during my childhood—and I recall my embarrassment the last time we saw that movie with Mom at the hospital because I was finally old enough to understand the fake orgasm scene with Meg Ryan at the restaurant. I also recall Dad putting on the movie the day after Mom's funeral and how he couldn't stop crying throughout.

"I'm sorry," Brooklyn says, probably spotting my expression. "I didn't mean to bring up your mom. Again."

"It's fine," I say, but I'm not sure if I sound persuasive enough.

Brooklyn clears her throat. "Do you mind if I play with Sally?"

I hand over a tiny slice of sashimi. "If you want a good start, give her this."

Brooklyn slowly walks over to the cat and proffers the treat.

Sally devours the fish, but her gaze doesn't warm up to the new human.

Brooklyn very pointedly blinks in slow motion at Sally.

Odd. But hey, Sally seems to like the gesture. She purrs and even rubs herself on Brooklyn's sleeve.

Seeing all that, Harry prances over and wags his tail at Brooklyn. *Dudette. I totally like to play too, bro. And if you could scratch behind my ear, that would be totally awesome sauce.*

Proving she can read Harry as well as I can, Brooklyn scratches behind his ears, making him quite happy. She then rubs his belly, which upgrades happy to ecstatic but makes Sally narrow her eyes.

"Watch out," I say. "The cat has a serious jealous streak." And, if I'm honest, I'm also a little jealous of all the PDA my dog is getting.

Fuck. What am I thinking?

Instead of slapping myself, I focus on finalizing our dinner. When it's ready, I set it on the table on a wooden tray in the shape of a boat.

"Wow," Brooklyn says, examining my work. "Are you sure you're not planning to open a restaurant?"

I grin. "Are you just flattering me because of the rescue?"

She plops into her chair and winces.

I frown. "Sunburn?"

Pretending she didn't hear, she grabs a pair of chopsticks, snatches a salmon piece from the boat, and dips it into the tiny bit of soy sauce that I poured for her.

"Put a little wasabi on top," I suggest just in time.

She does, then sensuously slides the morsel between her delectable lips.

Great. I'm hard now. And it gets worse because I could swear that she moans in pleasure as she starts to chew.

Maybe my dick is making me hallucinate this? But then her eyes roll back as if she's about to—oh.

"Very funny," I grumble. "We talk about *When Harry Met Sally*, and now you're replaying that famous scene."

Brooklyn swallows, her cheeks turning the color of the salmon. "What scene?"

Chapter Seven

BROOKLYN

That was a weak dodge. I know perfectly well what scene he is talking about: the one where Meg Ryan pretends to come. It's possible that I inadvertently acted it out, but in my defense, the sashimi is *that* good. The perfect blend of sweet, salty, and melt-in-your-mouth softness. Also, I haven't eaten all day. And he—

"Never mind." Evan clears his throat, clearly desperate to change the uncomfortable topic. As if coming to his rescue, the cat leaps onto the table, so he hands her a piece of tuna as he asks, "Do you have fur children of your own?"

Does Reagan count? "No," I reply out loud. Despite the long hair my son has decided to grow out, he's still not furry enough. "I do, however, want one," I continue. "Badly."

"You do?" Evan gestures at his dog. "Why don't you go to a shelter and rescue one?"

I sigh. "New York landlords like dogs and cats as much as the Grinch likes Christmas. Pets are almost never allowed in rentals."

"They sound worse than our HOA."

"That's a heavy indictment, coming from you." I grab more sashimi and cover it in wasabi.

A wet nose pokes me in the shin. I look down at Harry, who gives me a lolled-tongue grin.

"Can I give him some fish?" I ask Evan.

"Sure, but without any soy sauce or wasabi," he says. "And bear in mind, he'll pester you forever going forward."

I gleefully hand Harry a piece of squid.

The dog eats it with the same enthusiasm that I had, which is my cue to taste another morsel—and I struggle not to make orgasmic sounds yet again.

"You seem to like animals," Evan says. He makes it sound like a great compliment.

"I do," I say. "So much so that I wanted to become a veterinarian when I was a kid. When that didn't pan out, I became a pet groomer."

"Why didn't it pan out?" he asks.

Crap. I walked right into that one. If I want to come out as a mom, here's my chance. "Life got in the way," I say vaguely, taking the cowardly route. "What about you? Is managing an Airbnb your life's dream?"

He considers this over a couple of pieces of fish. "No. I want a farm. By the ocean. I want to grow my own food when I'm not surfing. I want Harry to be able to run free. Sally too. I'm increasingly realizing I want a simple life."

I smile. "Aside from the horrible chore of having to buy your own food, you seem to have a simple life already. Surf. Take care of the Airbnb. Play with fur kids. Did I miss anything?"

"Japanese food." He smiles once more, soothing all of my aches better than the Advil.

"*That* doesn't sound all that simple," I say.

His smile goes away, and so do its analgetic effects. Relatedly, the Advil must be wearing off. My cramps are coming back, and my skin is beginning to seriously burn. Sometime soon, I'll have to excuse myself and run to the car to get some more.

"What could be simpler?" He lifts a piece of yellow-tail with his chopsticks, his strong forearms distracting me for a second. "I can go fishing and then have a meal without having to cook anything."

Why, oh why did I think about the stupid sunburn? It's like it was waiting for me to do so before getting worse. "What about internet?" I ask Evan, doing my best to distract myself. "Would you have that on your hypothetical farm?"

He considers my question carefully. "I guess so, mainly to listen to music and watch movies."

I arch an eyebrow—which makes me realize my forehead is burned too. "What kind of movies and music?"

"Music by The Doors." He seems to inwardly smile. "And any movie with Faye Dunaway."

"Faye Dunaway?" I exclaim. "She was in my favorite movie of all time."

I also know about The Doors, mostly because my late grandmother had this to say about their lead singer, and I quote: "Jim Morrison was the most perfect human male to have ever walked this Earth."

"Which movie?" The blue-green specks in his eyes gleam.

"*Don Juan DeMarco,*" I say, flushing. There was a time when I felt about young Johnny Depp the way Grandma did about The Doors' singer.

"I saw that once," Evan says. "With my mom."

There I go again, reminding him about the tragedy in his life. Thankfully, he seems okay, so I carry on. Grabbing a piece of mackerel with my chopsticks, I say, "So, did you have a crush on Faye Dunaway as a kid or something?"

He flashes a grin. "Guilty. When I was fifteen, I saw her face on the cover of an old VHS tape and became obsessed for a while."

"Which film?"

"*The Thomas Crown Affair,*" he says.

"Oh." I resist the urge to scratch the burns on my back. "I've never seen that one. Only the version with Pierce Brosnan."

Evan smirks with disdain—a neat trick I'll need to practice in front of a mirror. "I don't understand why Hollywood is so obsessed with remaking movies that are perfectly fine as they are."

I shrug. "Sometimes they end up better than the original. For example, *Scarface* with Al Pacino was a remake."

He scoffs. "That's probably the only example in existence."

I cock my head. "There were many versions of *Dracula*, but Francis Ford Coppola's version from the early nineties is my favorite."

"That's not a remake," he says. "It's a screen adaptation, and if I ran the world, there'd be no movies based on books, period. They always suck."

My eyes widen. "If you ran the world, there wouldn't be *The Godfather*. Or *The Silence of The Lambs*. Or *Fight Club*."

He waves it off. "Lucky breaks."

"Then what about the recent *Dune* movie?" I say triumphantly. "It was awesome, even though it was both a book adaptation *and* a remake."

He sighs. "Are you sure you're not secretly a lawyer?"

"Are *you* sure you're not secretly a member of an HOA in Hollywood?"

"That's insulting," he says.

"And being called a lawyer is a compliment?"

He shakes his head. "I give up."

"Good." I grab more sashimi. "I accept your defeat."

He huffs. "There's a difference between losing an argument and not wanting to waste more time on it."

I roll my eyes. "'I don't want to waste more time on an argument' is what someone who's lost said argument usually says."

"Anyway," he says pointedly. "Am I still taking you to

the beach tomorrow? The one without waves. Or are you too traumatized after today? If so, we can start with Sealand. Or—"

"No, I can't." Why does it pain me to say the words so much? Could it be the quickly multiplying physical pains that I'm feeling?

He frowns. "Why not?"

"You're a busy homeowner. You can't use up so much of your valuable time on a renter."

Of course, if I'm honest, the bigger problem is that going on relaxing outings with Evan would feel too much like going on dates. In fact, this dinner feels like a date— or if looked at from a different angle, an imposition upon his Southern hospitality.

Yeah. I shouldn't have accepted this dinner. Jolene and Dorothy are my best friends, and I barely let myself accept this vacation from them. In Evan's case, I was the opposite of a friend when we met.

"I've already done all I needed to do for the rental," he says with a smile. "In terms of my other commitments, I don't plan to skip my volunteering gig tomorrow morning, but since you're on vacation, I'll probably be free by the time you wake up."

"You're a volunteer?" I ask.

"Lifeguard and surfing lessons," he replies. "But don't change the subject."

I purse my lips. "I don't need to change anything because the subject was already closed. You saved my life, not the other way around. If anyone should be doing any favors, it should be me doing something for you."

I drop my gaze to my plate, flushing again as I realize that I made that last bit sound like I was offering sexual favors. And... maybe I should?

No. At least not for a couple more days. Aunt Flo is still torturing me.

Wait. Period or no period, the answer is no, period.

Realizing I'm still staring down at an empty plate, I sneak a peek at my gracious host.

He looks more perplexed than intrigued, so he probably didn't take my words as an indecent proposal. Or he might be perplexed as to why I think he'd want said sexual favors.

"What if I were going to that beach anyway?" he asks. "What would be the big deal if you joined me?"

Before I can reply, my phone rings.

I snatch it out of my pocket immediately, in case it's the camp calling about Reagan.

Shit. The area code is local, so it just might be that.

"Hello?" I say, my heartbeat skyrocketing.

"Ms. Marquez," a familiar voice says. "This is Dr. Hugo."

My whole body relaxes, and I lean back into my chair—which causes the skin on my back to scream out in agony. "Hi, Doctor," I say with a wince.

My words seem to piss off Evan for some reason—that or he just put too much wasabi on his tuna.

"Please," the doc says. "Call me Vic."

I smile. "You call me Ms. Marquez, but I have to call you Vic?"

"Sorry," he says. "I'll call you Brooklyn from now on."

"That's a deal, Vic," I say. "Now, what's going on?"

"Oh, nothing," he says with a slight pause. "I just wanted to check how you're feeling."

"Wow," I say. "Back home, there are too many people around for the doctors to check on you once you leave their sight."

Vic chuckles. "Small towns do have their advantages."

"Seems like. But to get back to your original question, when it comes to any after-effects of the near drowning, I'm completely fine."

"Why does it sound like there's a 'but' in there somewhere?" Vic asks.

I look at Evan guiltily. "I'm sunburned."

Just as I was afraid, Evan's already-glowery expression gets glowery-er.

"I'm sorry," Vic says. "But on the bright side, that's a common malady for tourists, and all seem to survive. My medical advice would be to stay out of the sun for a few days and take ibuprofen as needed."

I sigh. "A few days?"

Sun is one of the major selling points of Florida. That and crazy stories about its denizens.

"Sorry. I'm sure you'll recover soon," Vic says.

"Thanks. I've got to run."

If I don't, Evan might start to breathe fire. He must be one of those people who hate cell phones at the dinner table.

"Ah, right," Vic says. "Later."

I hang up and meet Evan's surly gaze. "That was your friend."

"Vic and I are not *that* close," Evan grits out. "Not anymore."

Jeesh. Didn't he call him his buddy back at the hospital? "Is there a problem?"

"Vic is being rude," he says.

"How?"

"He saw us together, but he's hitting on you anyway."

Ah. So this is some male territoriality? "Vic was just being nice. Checking on my health."

"No," Evan says. "He was trying to ask you on a date."

He was? "I don't think so. Doctors aren't allowed to date patients."

Evan scoffs. "If Vic didn't date his patients, he'd never get a date in his life."

I roll my eyes. "You did tell him, 'We're not dating.'" And was almost insultingly adamant about that.

"Oh." Evan frowns. "I forgot."

"It's all moot anyway. If he asks me, I'll say no. I'm not into flings, which is the only thing possible when you're on vacation."

"That makes sense," Evan says and stuffs a large piece of sashimi into his mouth. As he chews, his expression grows calmer. Once he swallows, he asks, "Did you refuse my offer to take you places because you thought that *I* was asking you on a date? Because I wasn't. Unlike Vic, I never date tourists."

How flattering. "I refused for the exact reason I stated. I don't want to impose on your time. That's all." I don't even bother explaining that if he did deign to break his "no-tourists" rule, I'd say no anyway.

"Fine." His features soften. "How bad is your sunburn?"

I shrug, which ironically causes pain. "It's not fun."

"I'll make you my grandfather's sunburn poultice," he states. "It performs miracles."

I shake my head. "No, thanks. I've got Advil in the car. It will suffice."

"Is this the imposition business again?"

I stuff fish into my mouth to avoid replying.

Evan jumps to his feet. "I'm feeling a little sunburned myself," he says to no one in particular. "Excuse me while I make some poultice *for myself*."

Before I can object, he grabs a blender and rummages in his fridge and pantry.

Is that honey he's putting into the cup? Baking soda? Apple cider vinegar?

"Are you sure that's a poultice that you're making? And not, say, a cake?"

Ignoring my question, he walks over to an aloe plant that's sitting on a windowsill and clips a piece of it.

"Okay," I say. "That one makes sense."

He keeps adding ingredients: yogurt from the fridge, some dry leaves from a bag that says "Chamomile," and something green that—given his love of all things Japanese—is probably matcha.

"I'm going to taste delicious," I say without thinking. As soon as the words leave my mouth, I wince and pray that Evan either didn't hear me or doesn't have as dirty of a mind as I do.

Crap.

He halts his work and gives me an evaluating stare.

Or is it a hungry stare?

I guess he did hear?

Before I can decide, he goes back to his poultice making.

With her human distracted, Sally jumps onto the table and pointedly meows at me.

"Here." I give her a piece of sashimi.

She licks it and takes a dainty bite.

I feel a wet nose poking my calf. Glancing down at Harry, I give him a piece as well, which he devours like it's his last meal.

I join the fur kids in eating and soon realize I'm getting full. With a satisfied smile, I put down my chopsticks.

Shit. Smiling hurts the creases in my face, and moving my arms hurts the skin in the crook of my elbow.

Maybe I *do* need this poultice on top of the Advil. The pain is getting worse.

On the plus side, the cramps have eased, or it seems like they have in comparison to the misery my skin is experiencing.

A deafening roar erupts. It's the blender. The sound

makes it hard to focus on anything for the next few seconds. When it's over, Evan ladles the finished product into a jar and carries it to me. "Do you want me to help you apply it?"

Would that involve him touching me?

A huge part of me wants to say yes, but the more rational part opens my mouth to refuse—except it's too late.

Evan dips his finger into the thick liquid and draws a line with it on my forehead.

Holy aloe. This feels amazing, but probably not due to any medicinal properties of the ingredients. Evan's touch is hot and tingly on my skin, but the poultice he's left behind is cool and soothing.

"Should I continue?" he murmurs, his blue-green eyes glimmering down at me.

I nod silently. If I open my mouth, I might tell him to stop—or worse, to keep going and never stop.

He spreads the line he made on my forehead so that it covers all the surrounding skin.

I swallow hard. Is my forehead an erogenous zone, or has it turned into a clit? Merely soothing pain shouldn't feel this good.

Evan dips his finger back into the jar and tenderly applies the poultice to my right cheek.

Correction: my cheek is the erogenous zone. The brush of his fingers is disturbingly like a lover's caress, and it makes my head spin... and certain lower regions feel like they've gotten sunburned too. But in a good way.

Evan spreads the concoction over the rest of my cheek. I try very hard not to moan or let my eyes roll back. I do, however, turn my other cheek to him without being prompted—and more soothing pleasure is my reward.

Okay, my panties are officially wet.

This is not good.

Really not good.

I'm not into flings, and even less into one-night stands, but that is what my treacherous body seems to want.

But no. Even if I wanted to break my rules, there's the fact that Evan doesn't want a fling either, particularly with a tourist and doubly so with a breakfast thief like me. On top of that, there are practical considerations, like Aunt Flo and—

"Would you like me to put some on your back?" Evan murmurs.

Is he freaking kidding me? I have a strong will and all, but not *that* strong.

"I see," he says, clearly taking my dazed silence for refusal because he puts the lid on the jar of the poultice and hands it to me.

Instead of taking it, I blurt, "Yes."

Golly. My heart is hammering in my chest so fast I glance at Octothorpe Glorp to make sure I'm not experiencing arrhythmia.

One-twenty? It appears Evan's touch can put my body into the fat-burning mode faster than any elliptical machine.

My dear Precious, your body isn't just a temple, it's perfection on par with diamonds and Brussel sprouts. You need not gain or lose an ounce of that sweet nectar that is your fat.

Evan cocks his head, the way Harry might. "Yes?"

Sucking in a deep breath, I take off my coverup and thank the gods of propriety that I have bathing suit underneath. "Yes, please put the poultice on my back."

Chapter Eight

EVAN

My dick is so fucking hard I would not be surprised if I passed out from the shortage of blood to my brain. That shortage must also be the reason I offered to paw at Brooklyn's back after merely touching her face flooded me with more hormones than when I first got to third base.

And here is my punishment. Her almost-bare back in front of me, which, despite being red, is lithe and deliciously tempting.

Oh, well. I've made my bed. Now I must lie in it.

No. Can't think about beds, and especially things that happen in them. My throbbing cock doesn't need any more encouragement. As is, when I stick my fingers into the jar, I fantasize about them being inside Brooklyn's sweet pussy. And when I apply the poultice between her shoulder blades, I feel like I might burst.

I take a whiff of the poultice for strength and heroically proceed, manfully resisting random urges, like wanting to kiss her neck or to nibble on her earlobe. I'm no doctor like Vic, but even I know those things do not help with sunburn.

"So," I say, my voice more than a little hoarse. "What are some things that you're into, besides *Don Juan DeMarco*?"

"Why?" Her back muscles tense under my fingers, the way they would if she came all over my cock.

"Because I told you mine, but you never told me yours." But really because I need a distraction. If I'm lucky, she's into something unsexy, like the recent Godzilla movies.

"Papier-mâché would be my equivalent of your surfing," she says.

"Interesting." And more random than unsexy. "What else?"

Her shoulders bob just as I approach the right one with the poultice.

"I like Scrabble. And the *Harry Potter* series. And books by Judy Blume."

She sounds a bit belligerent as she says that. Does she expect me to make fun of the grade level of her reads?

"I love Scrabble. And I've read all of Rick Riordan," I admit reluctantly. "Recently."

How is it that I can see that she's smiling even though her back is to me?

"With your love of the ocean, you must relate to Percy Jackson," she says. "From the books, mind you, not the movie, Poseidon forbid."

I grin. "Percy and the Silver Surfer are my favorite fictional characters. From the books and comics, not the movies."

"Isn't the Silver Surfer a villain?"

Grr. Hollywood strikes again. "He had to serve an archvillain for a while. But eventually, he betrays said archvillain and saves Earth. Also, he was in a hero group once, called the Defenders. Not to mention—"

"You're a comic book nerd?"

Not even insults affect my dick. If anything, he might be usurping the blood that would've gone to my face. "There are comics like *The Sandman* that are high art, and I'm not ashamed to enjoy them. When I was a kid, they lured me into reading, and I'm sure they've done the same for many other kids. In any case, should a Potterhead really be throwing stones?"

Gooseflesh appears on her back—maybe over my words?

"'Nerd' isn't a negative word anymore," she says defensively.

"If you say so." I glide my finger down her spine and try to figure out how even her vertebra is so alluring and feminine.

"Can we move on, please?" she asks.

I apply some poultice under the strap of her bikini— fantasizing about unlatching the thing the whole time. "All I know is, you keep contriving ways to learn more about me than I know about you."

"Hmm," she says—and it could be my imagination,

but it sounds extra breathy, like she's on the verge of moaning.

It's official. My cock is now impacting my hearing.

"I'm into treasure maps," Brooklyn breathes out.

Huh. "That's a coincidence," I blurt. "It just so happens that my grandfather left me a treasure map."

Shit. Why would I tell her that? No idea, but it's safe to say a certain very erect body part is to blame.

She whips around to face me. "What do you mean?"

Seriously, what am I doing? "My grandfather was wealthy. When Mom died, he changed his will to be in my favor, and then passed away soon after that. That is how I ended up with my inheritance... which includes a treasure map."

She turns back. "Wow. What's the treasure?"

"No idea," I say as my hands glide down her back, slowly approaching the two delectable dimples at the base of her spine. "I couldn't crack Grandpa's code."

Hmm. *Grandpa's Code* could be a Dan Brown novel about Robert Langdon in retirement.

"Oh," she says. "Let me know if I can help. I'm good with anything treasure-map-related, including cyphers and codes, of course."

I don't reply because my fingers reach the dimples, and my balls get tight. I'd better move on, or else I might just get blue balls—something that until now, I thought was a convenient myth told by teen boys to teen girls.

Crap. Either by accident or driven by the will of my cock, the fingers of my right hand accidentally slip from the dimple and into Brooklyn's bathing suit bottom.

Once there, they lightly brush over the curve of her right butt cheek, giving my cock an apoplexy.

Not surprisingly, Brooklyn leaps to her feet and grabs her coverup.

"I'm so sorry," I say, feeling my face turn red. "That was an accident. The poultice is greasy, so my hand slipped."

I sure hope that's the truth because I wouldn't like myself if the explanation was anything else... which it could be.

"It's no big deal," she says breathlessly. "But I do think I've monopolized enough of your time at this point. Best if I apply the rest of the poultice myself."

Before I can voice another apology, or a rebuttal, she snatches the jar and sprints away as if a crazed sex maniac were on her heels.

I find my reflection in the microwave. Yep. My face has turned a shade that is not unlike that of Brooklyn's back—and yet, despite this clear evidence of blood flow elsewhere, I'm still hard as a rock.

The door slams in the distance.

Harry looks at me in confusion.

Human dude, where did the human dudette go? You seemed to be jelling, awesomely, and then poof.

On the table, Sally steals a piece of sashimi from the boat, then stares at me without even a hint of remorse.

It seems like our evil captor wanted to add another female creature to his evil harem. Luckily for her, she possesses opposable thumbs.

Shit. Brooklyn now thinks I'm a creepy perv, and she

might not be too far from the truth because here I am, walking to the bathroom to fist my cock.

Only after I come do I realize that I never bothered to wash the poultice from my hands and now have apple cider vinegar on my dick.

Chapter Nine

BROOKLYN

When I get to my rental, I pant like a dog in heat. I mean, an overheated dog—though that first bit could've been a Freudian slip because Evan's poultice application was the most sensual experience of my life.

How sad is that?

Jolene is right about my D deficiency. Maybe if I got laid once in a while, I wouldn't have reacted as I did.

And boy, did I react. When Evan ran his fingers between my shoulder blades, it took a herculean effort not to do something inappropriate, like touch myself.

Things just got worse from there, and his attempt at conversation didn't help. If anything, learning about his reading preferences made me want him more.

And then he touched my ass.

In an instant, I was ready to throw said ass at him. I even thought about practicalities, like the fact that my period shouldn't get in the way of anal.

Yep, that was an actual thought I had, even though I've never done anal.

That's when I knew I had to get the hell out of his house.

I sigh. At least the poultice seems to be working. My face and back are not hurting anymore, while the rest of me feels like it's being bitten by fire ants.

I toss the coverup aside and apply the poultice to my arms and legs. Unfortunately, I fantasize about Evan doing it as I go, and my horniness skyrockets again.

You know what? I'm going to do something about this.

Yeah. I wash my hands and head into the bedroom, where I close the blackout curtains, and without much preamble, go to work on my clit.

Boom.

I've always been quick to orgasm—when working solo, that is—but this is Guinness World Record fast. Seems like Evan's touch has really primed the whole system.

As soon as I'm done, I'm overcome with two urges: to shower and to sleep, ideally at the same time. Hey, at least I don't want a post-sex cigarette (like my ex—yuck) or an éclair (like Jolene). Not that I'm saying I slept with Jolene. She just volunteered the information.

Problem is, I shouldn't shower as that would remove the poultice.

That settles that.

I fiddle with Octothorpe Glorp to make sure my

morning alarm will not go off for the duration of my vacation.

My dear Precious, so long as I get to watch you sleep, I'm perfectly contented not to wake you—especially since your breath reaches the perfect bouquet of fragrance after nine hours and thirty seconds.

All righty then.

I close my eyes and pass out.

Chapter Ten

EVAN

I wake up super early and head to my volunteer gig.

When I get to the highway, my phone rings.

It's a video call from my long-distance drinking buddy, Mason. True to form, there's a shot of vodka in front of him.

"Are you free?" he asks.

"Where's the obligatory, 'Hey, Evan, how's it going?'"

"Hey, Evan, how's it going?" Mason says in a gravelly voice that, combined with his appearance, makes him look like a Viking... or an Asgardian from the Marvel movies. "Want to drink with me?"

"It's morning," I reply. As far as I know, Mason doesn't have a drinking problem; otherwise, I wouldn't have felt comfortable making our unusual drinking pact: when possible, we don't allow the other to drink alone. "Is everything okay?"

Guys in general—and Mason in particular—do not

chomp at the bit to talk about their feelings, but the morning drink speaks for itself.

"Is that a 'no?'" he asks.

"Time of the day aside, I'm clearly driving." New theory for his early drinking: his hockey team lost their game last night, the whole team went out to drown their sorrows, and this is a hair of the dog situation.

"So, it is a 'no.' Got it,'" Mason says and hangs up.

"Okay, Mason. Talk to you later. It was nice to catch up," I say to the already-disconnected phone. "It's not like I had anything to tell you about a fellow New Yorker."

Whatever. Instead of discussing the events of last night with a friend, I simply replay them in my head and wonder if Brooklyn will ever speak to me again.

Probably not, but if she does, how likely is she to bring up the treasure map stuff? She said she was into it, so it's possible, which means I'd better decide what to do in that scenario.

By the time I enter the camp, I have a plan, but I put it out of my mind for the moment because I see a group of campers waiting eagerly for me.

"Hello," I say to them, spotting a few unfamiliar faces. "I'm Evan. Just Evan. Not Mr. Evan, or Mr. Wilcox, which is my last name." I point at Harry. "He's Harry... and if you'd like, you can call him Mr. Harry."

A few kids chuckle, but most nod seriously, which means my dog *might* get called Mr. Harry by the time the day is through.

"Are you ready for your surfing lesson?" I say with a wide grin.

"Yes," they singsong in unison excitedly.

Cute. "Harry and I can't hear you. Are you ready for surfing?"

"Yes!" The excitement is through the roof this time, so I get them set up with safety gear and we head over to the water.

Time flies as the lesson proceeds, and the kids—and Harry—have a ton of fun.

One of the new students—a kid who reminds me of Macaulay Culkin from *Home Alone* but with long hair —walks over to me after the lesson is over and shuffles shyly from foot to foot.

"Hey, kid." I open my water bottle. "You did great today. You're a natural." And I mean it. He didn't drop in once, nor did he ditch his surfboard. He also listened to all the safety instructions patiently.

Harry also seems to like the kid because he wags his tail extra vigorously.

"Thank you," the kid says politely, continuing to shuffle from foot to foot like it's his job.

"Is there something on your mind?" I ask.

"Yeah," he says. "I have a personal question."

"What's up?" I take a sip from my bottle.

"Is it normal to grow hair down there?" He points at his crotch.

I almost choke on the water, but I don't, thank fuck. Having an adult die after asking such a question would guarantee this kid life-long therapy. And full-body laser hair removal.

"That's an interesting question," I say. "Have you asked your dad about it?" Because his father seems like a better-qualified person to answer than some dude he just met.

The kid sighs. "My dad left before I was born. It's just me and my mom, but I feel awkward asking her."

Maybe a guy with a vasectomy shouldn't judge and all, but his father sounds like an asshole. If, by some miracle, I did manage to get someone pregnant, I'd absolutely, positively stay in the child's life. And said child wouldn't even need to be as cute as this kid. They could be annoying and—

"Never mind," the kid says. "I'll just—"

"No, I was just thinking about the best way to answer," I say. "How old are you?"

"Seven," he says.

"And what's your name?"

He smacks himself on the forehead. "Sorry. I'm new here. My name is Reagan." He extends his little hand.

I shake the hand solemnly. "Okay, Reagan, here goes. Hair down there is normal, but it's rare at your age. Usually, it grows later, but it's all good. You're just ahead of everyone else."

The look of relief on his face tugs at something in my chest. "Thank you so much, Mr. Evan. At first, I thought it was normal, but then in the showers, I was the only one, so…"

"Understandable," I say. "And please, call me Evan."

"Okay," he says. "Evan. Thank you."

With that, he runs away—which causes Harry to look like he might give chase, but then he remembers his manners.

Cute kid. If that aforementioned pregnancy miracle were to come true, I'd want my child to be just like Reagan.

Better not think in that direction. I made my choice, and it was the right one—even if I did make it at a time when big decisions like that should not be made.

To distract myself, I focus on a topic I wouldn't have expected to think about in a million years: Grandpa's treasure map.

Chapter Eleven

BROOKLYN

My stupid phone is ringing in the far distance.

I glance at Octothorpe Glorp.

Wow. I clocked in a whooping twelve hours of sleep.

My dear Precious, watching your catatonic visage was a heavenly visual experience, but waking you up is transcendental for the olfactory senses.

The phone rings again. I pick it up and debate flinging it at the wall, but then I recall the three-hundred bucks I had to shell out to buy it, so I settle on giving the thing a glare.

Uncaring, the phone shows me why it's woken me up —a video call from Jolene.

I pick up. "What time is it?"

"It's eleven-thirty in the morning," she says, taking in my sleepy state with a grin. "Though, an argument could be made that it's not morning at all anymore, but early afternoon."

"Well, it's too early for arguments," I say. "What do you want?"

Before she can reply, I see that I'm getting a voice call from Dorothy.

"Let me call you back in a sec," I tell Jolene and switch to Dorothy's call. "Hey, I'm on a video call with Jolene. Can I—"

"I know," Dorothy says. "I'm supposed to be on it too, but I can't figure it out."

I resist the urge to tease. Dorothy's lack of skill with technology is legendary, and if she were calling me from a rotary phone—or a phone booth—I wouldn't be *that* surprised.

"How about you have Jolene work as your tech support?" I suggest. "Meanwhile, I'll brush my teeth."

"TMI," Dorothy says and hangs up.

I get up and rush through my morning routine, figuring I don't have much time before the call back.

Nope. As usual, I've underestimated Dorothy's lack of tech skills—or overestimated Jolene's ability to assist her. All I know is, I'm completely changed and thoroughly sun-blocked by the time they call me back.

"Hi, guys," I say to Jolene's face and Dorothy's forehead. "Check this out."

I take the phone over to the pool and show them the lake view.

"Wow," Jolene says. "It looks even better than in the pictures."

"Please don't do that again." Dorothy's forehead acquires a green hue. "That made me nauseated."

Aww, poor thing. I plop into a lounge chair and turn the phone camera onto myself—which, hopefully, is a bit less nauseating. "Thank you again, guys," I say earnestly. "This is the best gift ever."

The fact that I haven't had a chance to enjoy it yet isn't their fault, of course.

"You look like you've taken care of your vitamin D deficiency," Jolene says with narrowed eyes.

"I got sunburned," I say, pretending to misunderstand. The day I tell either of them that I masturbated last night will be the day I give myself a poodle haircut.

"Sunburned?" Dorothy's forehead wrinkles. "That can spike your chance of melanoma."

Great. "What if I put a poultice on it?"

"Doesn't matter," Dorothy says.

"What if I feel just fine today?" And I realize that I do. Completely fine. I can't believe that wasn't the first thing that I thought of this morning.

"Then maybe it wasn't a bad sunburn," Dorothy says. "Still, keep an eye on your moles."

"Eye on moles, check," I say. "Anything else?"

"Don't encourage her," Jolene says to me sternly. "I *know* you came last night, so spill."

Is she like Eleven from *Stranger Things*, but a pervert—able to remotely smell some sort of post-orgasm funk from a thousand miles away?

"There is nothing to say." Should I pretend the connection's cut off?

"I see," Jolene says. "You met a guy, but you didn't

hook up with him. You checked your own undercarriage instead."

WTF. Jolene is in real danger of getting experimented on by those creepy scientists from Hawkins Lab. "How could you know that?"

"And why do *I* have to know it?" Dorothy demands. "What a woman does below the belt is—"

"Shut up," Jolene cuts in. Narrowing her eyes at me, she says, "You have ten seconds to describe the guy, or I start detailing my Pornhub searches to Dorothy. One."

Seriously?

"Two. You know she might be scarred for the rest of her prudish life. Three."

Even though I'm morbidly curious about Jolene's scandalous searching, I take pity on Dorothy and tell them about meeting Evan and everything that followed —skipping only the part about the manual release when I got to my rental. Throughout, they both squeal— which is normal for Jolene but is as unnatural for Dorothy as ballet is for a hippopotamus.

"So let me get this straight," Jolene says. "He saved your life and made you a gourmet dinner, yet you still didn't give him any?"

Dorothy's eyebrows go high up on her forehead. "I can't believe I'm about to say this, but she's right. If any situation calls for lewd rewards, it's this one."

These two agree on something, *again*? Maybe pigs *can* fly—assuming their friend also goes on vacation and doesn't sleep with the first boar she meets.

Jolene chuckles. "Lewd? You make it sound like

Brooklyn should have her surfer come into a cup for a year before bukkakeing herself."

Hmm. That's *awfully* specific.

"Bu-what?" Dorothy demands. "Wouldn't she get sick from drinking something with protein after collecting it for that long?"

Jolene purses her lips. "Not if she freezes it every time to avoid spoilage, obviously. Then, on B-day, she could defrost it all and gulp it down while he watches. Still more hygienic than a gangbang."

"Gulp?" Dorothy's forehead seems to permanently develop a wrinkle. "As in—"

"Even if I were to offer, Evan would refuse any lewd rewards," I interject. "He said he doesn't do anything with tourists, and that's what I am."

I don't mention the practicalities of being on my period, as that would sound like I've seriously considered doing things with Evan, which I totally haven't.

Having said that, my period does seem to be over today—a bit early too, probably because my uterus likes Evan so much it's decided not to stand in the way of any lewd rewards.

"Show me a guy not into bukkake, and I'll show you an asexual," Jolene says. "Guys *love* to get cum into and onto their sexual interests as often as possible." She locks eyes with me. "Are you sure he didn't put some into that poultice?"

"I don't think so," I say. "I would've noticed." And maybe not minded.

"I think I'm going to have nightmares." Dorothy

finally moves the phone a bit lower, so you can see the fear in her eyes. "If this was you filtering yourself, how bad are your Pornhub searches?"

Great question. Before I can also ask, a cat jumps onto my chaise, scaring the bejesus out of me—and I don't even know what a bejesus is.

"Sally?" I say, slowly blinking in order to soothe the cat—and wishing someone could do that for me.

"Sally?" Dorothy says. "As in, *his* cat?"

"Yeah," I say. "One and the same."

"Watch out," Dorothy says worriedly. "Cats can give you T. gondii."

"What's that?" I ask. It sounds like "Gandhi, I", which could be an autobiography—except for the bit where cats can give it to you. Speaking of stories about great men, I wonder if Evan hates biopics as much as book adaptations? If so, I'll need to make sure to point out to him how amazing the Gandhi movie with Ben Kingsley is.

Wait, why am I planning conversations with Evan? I probably won't see him again.

"The 'T' stands for toxoplasma," Dorothy says.

"And that's supposed to explain it?" I do file the word away, though, as one day it might score me twenty-one points in Scrabble.

"It's a parasite." Dorothy enunciates the word with way too much relish. "If it's in your brain, it makes you like cats and leads to other risky behaviors."

"How is liking cats a risky behavior?" I stare at Sally and wonder if I already have said parasite—because I like this cat way too much, considering our short acquaintance.

"Didn't I just say?" Dorothy grumbles. "Cats can give you T. gondii."

Is that circular logic, or is that what the cat's brain parasite *wants* me to think?

Jolene fakes a yawn. "I've got to say, the cat thing is uncreative. Evan wants pussy, so he's using pussy to get it? If I were you, I'd get a pet rooster and send him to Evan's house."

"That's dumb," Dorothy says sternly. "The cat would eat the rooster."

That's what's dumb about her idea?

"The pussycat is with Brooklyn, so the cock would be safe," Jolene says. "Keep up."

"I'm going to go deal with Sally," I state firmly.

"Fine, but keep us posted." Jolene waggles her eyebrows libidinously.

"And stay out of the sun," Dorothy says with motherly concern that's in sharp contrast to my other friend's antics.

"Bye." I hang up, then face the cat. "Hi. How did you get in here?"

Sally blinks at me, then leaps into my lap.

Okay.

Petting her soft fur, I look around.

Yep. I'm in an aluminum cage covered by still-intact netting on all sides—a pool enclosure designed to keep bugs and animals away.

Maybe she got into the house first and then got in here? But houses are also designed to keep things out.

"How did you get in here?" I ask again softly.

Sally purrs in reply.

"Out of the two of you, you should have been called Harry, as in Houdini."

"Sally!" Evan shouts somewhere in the distance.

"She's here," I yell back and get a glare from the cat for my troubles.

Evan approaches from the lake side, and when he notices me holding Sally, the relief on his face is quickly replaced by a puzzled expression that perfectly matches the one that was very recently on my face.

Sigh. He probably didn't send Sally here as a ploy, as Jolene insinuated.

"How did you get in there again?" Evan demands, locking eyes with the cat.

Is that a smug expression on Sally's face?

"Did you see her since I left yesterday?" I ask. "Maybe she snuck out between my legs as I was leaving, and then got in here the same way."

I'm glad Jolene didn't hear me say "between my legs" because she'd wax ecstatic about "pussy" for an hour.

Evan shakes his head. "A good theory, but Sally was home this morning when I fed her."

"Here." I offer Evan the cat—once again, I can picture Jolene saying something about me offering him pussy.

As he takes the furry creature, his fingers brush mine, generating a major flashback to yesterday, when they touched my face, back, and—albeit briefly—my butt.

Holding the cat, Evan gently caresses her fur.

Huh. She purrs much louder for him than she did for me. Then again, who can blame her? Also, Jolene has officially taken up residence inside my brain, like Dorothy's *T. gondii*. Why else would I be thinking the phrase "gently caresses the pussy?"

"How is your skin feeling?" Evan asks.

Tingly. Fluttery. And that's just the fingers that came into contact with his. When it comes to the skin in my nether regions, it's flushed, humid, and thirsty.

"The poultice worked," I manage to say. "I'm good as new."

Evan narrows his eyes. "Hopefully, this doesn't mean you're planning on sleeping on the beach again?"

Before I can provide an indignant reply, my phone rings.

Huh.

"Hello, Vic," I say after I pick up. "Are you checking on my health *again*?"

At the good doctor's name, Evan's features turn stormy.

"Hi, Brooklyn," Vic says. "How are you feeling?"

"Completely recovered," I say pointedly. "So... you're officially free from having to check up on me."

"That's great to hear," Vic says. "But I wasn't *just* calling to check on you."

"Oh?" Was Evan right when he said Vic wanted to ask me out?

"I was wondering if you'd like to get a drink with me tonight," Vic says.

"Like a date?" I blurt, still unable to believe a hot doctor would be interested in me after seeing me looking like a drowned crab in a hospital gown.

Evan's jaw ticks.

"A date would be great," Vic says.

"In that case, I'm sorry," I say, and mean it. "I don't date when I'm on vacation."

Could Evan's twitching jaw be coding threats to Vic in Morse Code?

Vic sighs. "It was worth a shot."

"I guess," I say. "But shouldn't you have cleared this with your *friend* Evan before asking? You did see us together and all."

"He said you two were friends," Vic says defensively.

"True, he did say that," I say pointedly, making sure Evan hears. "I was just wondering if there's a bro code that still prohibits your behavior."

Vic scratches his head so hard that I can hear it. "I might have to buy Evan a beer," he says.

I look at Evan's disgruntled expression. "Make it a case of beer."

"Okay," Vic says. "But if you change your mind, give me a call."

On that, I hang up and look challengingly at Evan, daring him to say anything along the lines of "I told you so."

"Would you like to see that treasure map?" Evan says instead, and it's so unexpected that I blink stupidly at him before I recall him mentioning a treasure map he got from his grandfather.

"Would I like to see a treasure map?" I repeat, my excitement growing. "Is oxyphenbutazone a good Scrabble word?"

Yes, that's an actual word. Had I become a vet, I would have probably prescribed it for horses who need pain relief or fever reduction.

A smile touches the corners of Evan's eyes. "When I would play Scrabble with my mom, surfing jargon and pharmacological terms were forbidden—the latter became a rule after she used that exact word." The smile dissipates, tugging on something inside me. "She was a pharmacist."

Should I tell him that I usually play Scrabble with my son, and that we have custom rules too, some really whacky?

Evan turns toward the door he came in from. "I'm going to go get the map and the cypher. I'll be back in a few minutes."

There's a cypher? How exciting. When I was a teen, I encoded my diary with a secret code that no one has been able to crack—and I know that my overbearing parents tried their damnedest.

Wait. Why am I wasting time?

As I rush back to my rental, I quickly call Reagan at the camp and get an earful of the fun he's having, which, coincidentally, includes a scavenger hunt. When I get a chance to speak, I mention I'm doing something like a scavenger hunt myself, and he demands to know more, so I tell him about the clues and everything else.

In the end, he concludes his hunt was much more fun, and who am I to argue with the wisdom of a seven-year-old?

As we talk, I spruce up my hair and apply a copious amount of makeup.

It's not for Evan, obviously. I just want to look and feel good on my vacation.

Yeah, that's my story, and I'm sticking to it.

Just as I gush to Reagan about how much I miss him —and right before he chastises me for being too gooey— there's a knock on the door.

Shit.

"Bye, honey, I love you," I say and hang up.

Pulling the door open, I gape at Evan—who has somehow gotten handsomer in the short time he wasn't here.

Then it hits me.

He's put some product in his hair and has swapped his T-shirt for a dressy Hawaiian shirt... which he's only buttoned midway.

Wow. Isn't it criminal to look good in that? What would happen if he ever wore a suit? Would I go blind from his radiance?

"I've got us both some lunch." Evan waves a big bag in front of me. "Treasure maps don't like to be figured out on an empty stomach."

I'm still a bit stunned as he walks inside and sets the food on the kitchen table.

"Wait a second." I study the food carefully. "Isn't this—"

"Japanese tapas." He makes air quotes around the second word. "I happen to know that you like them, so..."

My stomach growls.

How ladylike.

I join Evan at the table and swiftly swallow a few yummy morsels to make sure my stomach stays silent from here on out.

"Where's the treasure map?" I demand after the edge of my hunger is blunted.

Evan spreads two papers in front of me, looking rather reluctant for some reason.

Is he afraid I'll crack the code and steal his treasure?

Whatever. I focus on the papers: one a map, one a page ripped out of a notepad, both weathered and smelling vaguely familiar. Something about their scent reminds me of New York, but I can't place it.

On the map is a hand-drawn penis shape that I recognize. "This is the state of Florida," I exclaim.

"That's as much as I was able to recognize," Evan says.

I frown. The map isn't to scale, and there's no X marking the spots, like on a traditional treasure map. And instead of a legend of names and places, to one side of the map are numbers going from north to south and from west to east. There are also numbers on the other paper, the one that I presume is the cypher.

I point to the map. "Could this be a number grid,

like in cartesian geometry? And those numbers the coordinates on said grid?" I gesture at the numbers on the cypher.

Evan takes out a folder that is full of copies of the treasure map, each littered with dots. "I tried plotting the numbers, but there doesn't seem to be a pattern as such."

Hmm. I scan the numbers on the cypher, the taste of my yummy food growing distant.

"Have you tried converting these numbers to letters of the alphabet?"

Evan shakes his head. "I'm not really a fan of this sort of thing."

Hey, if he were, he'd be too perfect and even harder to resist.

Eating my food ever more mindlessly, I scan the first line of numbers: "151317761565177618301776."

"I could consider each number to be a corresponding letter in the alphabet," I say, more to myself than to Evan. "But there's no obvious divider number, like a zero, so I can't tell if the first two numbers are 1 and 5 or 15."

"Right," Evan says.

"It's a safe bet that the clusters of numbers will not form something higher than twenty-six, since there are only that many letters in the alphabet."

"Obviously," he says.

"So, taking just the first four numbers, I either get 'aeac,' 'aem,' or 'om'"

"'Om' is the sacred sound they make in meditation," Evan says.

"Right, but if I keep going in that way, I get 'omq' or 'omagg.'"

He scratches his head. "Those aren't words."

"Nope." Yet I keep going and write down every variation of the gibberish. This is when I notice something. The string "AGGF" turns up a lot, so I look it up on my phone.

Hmm. There's a German medical society promoting women's health that uses that acronym. As in, a dead end.

Or maybe not. Looking more closely, I realize that the string's corresponding number, 1776, appears three times in one line.

I look up that number and then feel stupid for doing so. I studied this back in school. 1776 is year one for the United States as a nation.

Could this be the delineator? And could the other numbers be important years?

Yes! I look up 1513 and learn that it was the year Michelangelo painted the Sistine Chapel ceiling.

Could Evan's grandfather be making a Ninja Turtle reference here?

Doubt it.

Henry the VIII also took the throne that year.

Something to do with multiple marriages?

Unlikely.

It was also the year when Machiavelli wrote *The Prince.*

Hmm. Did Evan's grandfather want to brag about how Machiavellian his cypher is?

Wait.

1513 was also the year when a conquistador named Juan Ponce de León first sighted and claimed a certain land for his home country of Spain.

A land that he named after the Spanish word for "flowery"—*florido*—and that we now know as Florida.

As in, the penis shape on the map! I have to be on the right track here.

Using this info and the year 1565 leads me to a specific location in Florida, one that is actually a short drive away from Palm Islet: *St. Augustine.* A city that, according to Wikipedia, is "the oldest continuously occupied settlement of European origin in the continental United States." It was founded in 1565.

Continuing in this vein, I soon figure out a more exact location within St. Augustine: the campus of what is now Flagler College, but which used to be a hotel named Hotel Ponce de León, founded by a Gilded Age industrialist named Henry Morrison Flagler who was born in 1830.

Brimming with excitement, I move on to the next line of numbers when Evan clears his throat.

Shit. I forgot he was even here—and given how hot this man is, that speaks volumes.

"You look like you've got something," he says, studying me intently.

"I do," I say and tell him about my findings.

"Boy, do I feel dumb," he says after I'm done. "I went to Flagler College."

"You did?"

"Yeah," he says. "Majored in marketing. Can't you tell?"

"Totally," I say. "You sold me on that poultice, that's for sure."

I really hope he doesn't ask me about my college experience. To answer that, I'd have to talk about my pregnancy and—

"Do you want to go chase down this clue?" Evan asks, surprising me.

I grab the last of the Japanese food and stuff it gracelessly into my mouth—a kind of Twix commercial moment to give me a chance to gather my thoughts.

"I'll split the treasure with you," Evan says, and I think he's trying to sound seductive. Or I hope he is because otherwise, I'm now wet for no reason.

"Split the treasure?" I finally manage to say.

He stands up. "Fifty-fifty?"

"No. We can't do that. It was your grandfather. This is your birthright we're talking about." Feeling a little wobbly, I nevertheless get to my feet.

"And I can't have you working for me for free."

"So give me like five percent," I suggest. "Not half."

"Firstly, splitting things in half is easier," he says. "Secondly, wouldn't you work that much harder for a bigger cut?"

Should I tell him I'd help out for free?

"Look, I have to insist," he says.

"Fine." Mostly because I'm just too out of it to argue further. I can always refuse the treasure once and if we find any."

"Oh, I do have one further condition," he says.

Marry him?

"You have to put on sunblock," he says.

Oh. How mundane. "Sure." I walk over to the counter, grab the tube, and apply the cream to my arms and legs.

When I look up, Evan's eyes are gleaming. "What about your back?"

Oh. Right. There's a low cut on my back. Knowing I'll regret it, I hand him the sunblock and turn.

By all the hormones. Evan's fingers brush the nape of my neck, then slide down gently and caress the skin between my shoulder blades.

If I thought I was hot and bothered by his seductive voice or the poultice application, I didn't know the meaning of the words. All I want to do is excuse myself to go to the bathroom and scoop water out of my lady boat, like a perv. Alternatively, I want to drag him into the bedroom and enact a different kind of treasure hunt with him there, one where he—

"There you go." He removes his hands from my skin, allowing some semblance of coherent thought to return —though not much.

In a haze of lust, I follow Evan to his car, and we head out to St. Augustine via the scenic A1A highway.

"Was your grandfather a big fan of Florida trivia?" I ask when some of my wits return.

"Big time," Evan says. "And he passed that down to me."

I tear my eyes from the ocean to regard him skeptically. "You know Florida trivia?"

If so, why hasn't he cracked the treasure map code?

"I do." He glances at me, looking cocky. "Go ahead. Test me."

Since I can never refuse a challenge, I pull out my phone and do a few searches.

"Tell me some fast-food facts related to Florida," I demand.

"Is orange juice junk food?" he asks. "Because seventy percent of US oranges come from here."

"Fruit is like the opposite of junk food, and I asked about fast food, which is slightly different. I'll count that answer as a loss."

He purses his lips, making me want to kiss them. "I've always been told that orange juice is pure sugar and therefore junk. But fine. What's a fast-food fact about Florida?"

"The first ever Burger King was founded in Jacksonville," I say. "Moving on... What weather pattern is your home state famous for?"

"Thunderstorms," he says. "We have the most thunderstorm activity of any state."

Hmm. I was expecting him to say it's the most hurricane-prone state, but a quick search confirms that his answer is right also.

We continue in the same vein, and he does know his stuff, like the fact that Florida is the flattest state in the US, and that Native American tribes had been living in the

Florida region for several thousand years before the arrival of the Europeans. Also, that Florida officially became part of the US in 1821, and that it's the only place in the world where you can find both crocodiles and alligators in the wild.

"We're almost there," Evan says. "I'm going to look for parking."

"Okay." I pay attention to our surroundings, and I'm glad I do because the architecture around us is very neat and what you would expect to see in the oldest city in the United States.

"Is that a river?" I ask, pointing at the majestic body of water nearby, one with a pretty bridge going over it.

"That's the Intracoastal Waterway," Evan says with such pride you'd think he filled the thing with water himself. "It runs three thousand miles across multiple states."

"Huh."

"Yeah, and that's the Bridge of Lions." He gestures to the right at the pretty bridge, one that not very surprisingly features lion statues. "Had we stayed on A1A, we would have eventually crossed it."

"Awesome. Will we walk over it to get to our destination?"

"No," he says. "But we can go for a stroll there later if you wish. After the sun sets."

Hmm. That sounds a bit too suddenly romantic, but I don't rule it out. Despite it being a bad idea for us to engage in something resembling a date activity, I owe it to Jolene and Dorothy to relax on this vacation, and an evening stroll across that bridge might just do the trick.

"Okay, since I'm playing tour guide, over there is the Castillo de San Marcos." Evan gestures to the right again. "It was built in 1695 and was declared a National Monument almost a hundred years ago."

"Damn." It's an honest-to-goodness castle. I'm not sure why I find that surprising, considering the "Castillo" bit. "Your grandfather should've hidden the treasure clue in the castle instead of at a college that used to be a hotel. That's what Dan Brown would have done."

Then again, in a Dan Brown book, an albino priest would be waiting for us at the Castillo, biding his time with self-flagellation or watching *The Emoji Movie*.

"The college is open to the public," Evan says. "Castillo, on the other hand, requires tickets. Despite being wealthy, my grandfather was thrifty. Or as he'd say, one caused the other."

"But how much is a ticket?" I ask.

Evan grins. "Fifteen bucks. 'Thrifty' might be a bit of an understatement when describing Gramp."

"Huh. At that price, I want to check it out, after we get our clue."

"Gladly," he says. "It's been a while since I've been there."

Shit. I've just strong-armed him into another date-like activity.

But Evan doesn't seem to notice or care because he keeps pointing out more attractions, like *Ripley's Believe It or Not*—a place Reagan would love—and the historic St. George Street.

Speaking of said street, as soon as we park, we take it to get to our destination.

Wow. This reminds of New York's most touristy spots. There are snacks on every corner, various bars and restaurants, clothing shops, and people dressed in pirate costumes. Okay, that last bit isn't like New York. In New York, we have unauthorized Disney characters.

"Want to try the best ice pop, ever?" Evan asks.

"Would oxazepam be a good Scrabble word?" It's a medication used to treat anxiety—for people, not horses.

Smiling, Evan herds me to make a turn. "I thought we already agreed not to use pharmacological terms in Scrabble."

Ah. Right. "Is this the place?"

Nodding, he opens the door and challenges me to pick the Watermelon Jalapeño Margarita pop, so I do.

Scanning the other flavors, I see Peanut Butter Apple Pie, which would've been Reagan's pick, for sure.

Though it seems like a weird combo, I love my ice pop, but Evan's company might have something to do with that.

As he leads me down St. George Street, he tells me about the hilarious flavor combos he would have the ice pop place make if *he* were in charge. Flavors that include —but are not limited to—chicken tempura, spicy tuna, and sea urchin gonads.

"That marketing degree is clearly being put to good use," I say. "Ice pops that taste like Japanese food. Why not Italian? Mexican? Indian?"

"I did use my degree." He licks his pop, which is

extremely distracting. "You've got to give people a product that makes them feel like a part of the tribe. A foodie tribe, in this case."

"More like a Japanese food addict's tribe." I dodge a leaflet-carrying pirate. "More importantly, how would you even turn deep-fried—not to mention breaded—chicken into an ice pop?"

"Blend it with milk first?" He shrugs. "I'm just the marketing guy. I'd leave it to the chef to figure that part out."

We turn from St. George Street onto a small park, where Evan gives me a choice: check out some famous spots first or head to the college.

I choose to sightsee, and we swing by three places: Cathedral Basilica, the Casa Monica Hotel, and the Lightner Museum. As a result, I now have a new vision for my dream wedding: a ceremony at that cathedral with a reception in the courtyard of the museum, followed by a honeymoon at that hotel.

Yeah, right. That's as likely as Evan being the groom.

"Ready?" Evan gestures at a gorgeous castle-like building across the street from the museum.

I nod, and we cross the street. I scan my surroundings, channeling my inner Robert Langdon... to no avail. As far as this campus goes, I don't see any clues—just amazing photo opportunities, especially by the fountain in the courtyard.

"Can we go inside the building?" I ask.

Evan says yes, and we go in. Instantly, I feel like I've

been magically teleported to the Hogwarts School of Witchcraft and Wizardry.

"Wow." I gape at the domed ceiling. "Maybe your grandfather was right to plant the clue here."

Speaking of the clue... I intensely study the paintings, run my hand along the wooden rails to feel for any nicks or scratches, and pore over the patterns on the floor, trying to decipher if they have any meaning.

Nope. I still have no idea where the clue is hidden, or whether it even exists.

"I can get you farther into the building," Evan says when I complain. "I still have connections here."

"Yes, please."

A tour guide takes us through the library, dining hall, and various common areas, all beautifully adorned with either mosaic floors, stained glass windows, or gorgeous chandeliers. After a few hours of searching every nook and cranny for clues and badgering our poor tour guide with a million questions, I officially give up. As a consolation prize, Evan offers to take me to a restaurant that makes everything from scratch with seasonal ingredients and local produce.

———

"I just don't get it," I say as our Maltese-looking waitress leaves our orders in front of us. "Could it be that I didn't crack your grandpa's code properly?"

Evan shrugs. "Maybe you need to decode the rest of the paper?"

Great idea. I pull out said paper and get to work—only to learn that the next string of numbers is a completely different location elsewhere in Florida: the Vizcaya Museum and Gardens in Miami.

Hmm. Using my phone, I learn what I can about the spot in question, but all that gets me is a desire to visit.

"We can drive down there tomorrow," Evan says when I tell him what I've found. "We can stay at my friend's house overnight."

Overnight? It sounds tempting for all the wrong reasons.

"Let me see where else these clues point to," I say instead, ignoring my delicious-smelling food as I continue decoding.

Aha. The next line of numbers leads to the Sunken Gardens in St. Petersburg, and the one last line corresponds to the Florida Caverns State Park in Marianna.

"How are these connected?" I ask, frowning.

Evan glances at our quickly cooling meals. "Any chance you'll start eating soon, so I can join you?"

Oh, crap, I didn't even notice he was being a gentleman.

I put a forkful of risotto into my mouth. "Damn. That's really good."

Evan reaches with his fork. "Mind if I try it?"

I flush. Somehow, his words sound sexual.

"Sure. Can I taste yours?"

His eyes gleam. Did *my* words sound sexual this time?

"Please." He gestures at his blackened pasta. "Enjoy."

I stab my fork into his food, and it turns out to be even better than mine.

Or so I think.

He claims that he likes my dish more.

"How about we swap?" I ask.

He agrees, so I grab his plate and give him mine. On a lark, I swap our identical waters too, and my reward is his smile.

Only after it's all done do I realize that this is something a married couple would do, not whatever we are to each other.

"You know," Evan says. "If I had known you'd get this obsessed with the treasure map, I wouldn't have involved you in the hunt."

Oh. "Am I bad company?"

He shakes his head. "It's not that. You're on vacation, but I don't think you've done any relaxing today."

I consider this as I chew my pasta. "The truth is," I say after I swallow, "solving puzzles is equivalent to a spa day for me."

And that's the truth, just not the whole truth—which is that I've been laser focused on the treasure map to distract myself from Evan. I don't want to pay attention to how sweet he is, showing me all the sights. And how he's so hot that all the female tourists—and some male ones too—gawk at him everywhere we go.

To put it another way, he's correct. Despite the fun, I'm tenser than I was back in New York. Which really blows because relaxing was at the top of my to-do list—

and not just for myself, but also for Jolene and Dorothy, who invested money for me to do that one simple task.

That settles it. From this moment on, I'll fucking chill out.

I stick another bite of heavenly pasta into my mouth and chew it slowly, mindfully, contemplating the local ingredients the chef used.

Nope. As good as the food is, it's not cutting it. Something stronger is required, like chocolate, or cheese, or Evan's tongue on my clit.

"Would you like a drink?" the waitress asks suddenly, and it's like an answer to my unsaid prayer.

You can say all the negative things about alcohol until the cows come home from the beach, but there's one thing it's very good at: taking the edge off.

Chapter Twelve

EVAN

Ten seconds earlier

"The truth is," Brooklyn says, "solving puzzles is equivalent to a spa day for me."

I stare at her, my heart pounding faster. It's as if she's spoken my thoughts. Though I'm not a huge fan of spas, this is the most fun I've had in years, and I've been to St. Augustine a million times before.

Shit. What am I thinking? She's a tourist. She's transient. And even if she were local, she seems like the type of person who'd want a family one day, which is not something I can give her.

"Would you like a drink?" the waitress asks, startling me.

I expect Brooklyn to refuse, but she nods overeagerly. "I saw a cocktail with rum on the menu earlier." Turning to me, she guiltily adds, "This town seems to be pirate-themed, so..."

"I know which drink you mean," the waitress says approvingly.

Why did I assume Brooklyn doesn't drink alcohol? No idea, but I can't let her drink alone.

"Do you still serve that cocktail with St. Augustine vodka?" I ask the waitress. Turning to Brooklyn, I explain, "There's a local distillery here."

"We do," the waitress says.

"Actually, I'll have what he's having," Brooklyn says.

Smiling knowingly, the waitress nods and rushes away.

"What were we talking about?" Brooklyn asks.

I eat another spoonful of the delicious risotto. "That you need to relax," I remind her pointedly.

She sighs. "Hence the drink."

Ah. That makes sense. And it will take more than one, I suspect. So be it. I take out my phone and type out a quick text.

"Who are you talking to?" Brooklyn asks when I look up. She sounds a lot more casual than her narrowed eyes would imply.

What have I done now? Is she like me and doesn't like texting at the table? If so, that's legit.

"I want to make sure Boon and Bonnie can pick up my car and give us a ride back," I explain. "I don't drink and drive."

Taking that as her cue, the waitress brings our drinks.

Brooklyn takes a sip and raises her perfect eyebrows appreciatively. "I didn't realize I'd be putting you out."

"You're not." I sip my drink. "I could use one of

these as well, and as to Boon and Bonnie, they are much cheaper than an Uber would be."

Brooklyn frowns. "I thought they were friends doing you a favor. With money involved, you have to let me pay half of it."

I put my drink down. "We're not talking about a lot of money. I'm not sure if you noticed it, but those two were sitting on a junkyard couch. On the beach."

"Still," she says stubbornly, "I want to pay you back for getting my car home the other day and for today. Also, in case you're thinking about picking up the check here, don't."

I blow out an exasperated breath. "Do you *mean* to sound insulting when you say things like that?"

Her eyes widen. "Insulting?"

"Say I wanted to make a phone call and asked you for a quarter: would you lend it to me or give it?"

She cocks her head. "A quarter?"

"For a payphone."

She grins. "That's what I thought you meant. Has walking around this very old city somehow made your brain think we're in the nineties?"

I take a big gulp of my drink. "It's a hypothetical payphone."

"Even hypothetical payphones are long gone," she says. "Everyone nowadays carries one of these amazing technological marvels that not only take selfies but also make phone calls."

"Fine," I say with an eyeroll. "How about this: if you

let me use your cellphone, would you make me pay you back for the minutes I used up?"

She sips her drink smugly. "I have unlimited calling."

"What if you gave me a piece of gum? Would you let me pay you back for it?"

She grins. "Is that a hypothetical hint that I have bad breath, or that you do?"

"You know what I mean," I growl.

"I do," she concedes. "But your logic doesn't apply. I saw the prices on this menu."

Should I tell her that the prices on this menu are like the cost of gum to me? No. I don't want to sound braggadocious. That's the same reason I lied to her about having a friend in Miami instead of telling her that I plan to rent my favorite Airbnb. Now I'll also say I have friends in St. Petersburg and Marianna—all wanting me to "housesit" for free.

"How about we play Scrabble to settle this?" I offer, hoping she's buzzed or competitive enough to agree.

"You brought Scrabble tiles with you?" She looks at me like I've grown a cock on my forehead—and I hope I haven't because that's just an extra cock to get hard in her presence.

"Everyone nowadays carries one of these amazing technological marvels that not only take selfies and make phone calls, but also let you play Scrabble." I can't resist a self-satisfied smirk.

Blushing fetchingly, she takes a gulp of her drink. "How do I know you won't lose on purpose?"

"I don't need to. The agreement will be: if I win, I get

the check, and if—and this is purely hypothetical—I lose, we split it."

Her eyes gleam. "You're on."

Someone is overconfident in her skills.

We take our phones out and set everything up in the Scrabble app before beginning our epic battle of words.

I quickly take the lead, and by the time we're done with our food and desserts (along with three drinks for her and six for me), my victory seems almost guaranteed.

"This isn't fair," she says, her words a little slurred. "I always play with modified rules and more tiles."

"Seriously? I let you get away with using the word 'pharmacology,' even though we agreed not to use pharmacological terms."

She rolls her eyes. "I'll say it again, 'pharmacology' itself isn't a pharmacological word."

"And I say if a noun is a noun, why is 'pharmacology' not a pharmacological term?" Shit. I'm not actually sure that made sense.

"I can use that 'logic' too. The word 'curse' isn't a curse word," Brooklyn says stubbornly. "And the word 'animal' isn't itself an animal."

This is the most frustrating thing about women. They tend to be too good at arguments. "You know what? How about this: pharmacological terms are henceforth allowed. I'll still beat you."

"You sure?" she asks, looking suspiciously innocent. "How about chemical names?"

I assess the situation: my tiles are gone, and I've got a huge lead. "Do your worst."

With a triumphant grin, Brooklyn plays a word I have never even heard before: benzoxycamphors.

What the fuck? With that one move, she runs out of tiles and forms three other words, getting an obscene score in the process.

"I win!" she squeals.

Oh, yeah. That too.

I check if the word is a real one, and yep, it's actually famous for being a Scrabble word that yields an absurd number of points—which is how she must've learned about it.

"You cheated." I bet the slurring was a ruse too, to trick me into lowering my guard, which I did.

"Is someone a sore loser?" She makes a drink gesture at the waitress.

"I demand a rematch."

"A deal is a deal," she says. "We split the bill."

I sigh. "Look, I was so confident that I'd win, I ordered more drinks than I would have otherwise. It wouldn't be fair for you to pay for half of them."

She rolls her eyes. "Who sounds insulting now?"

"It's not the same."

The waitress brings Brooklyn's drink and asks me if I want another too.

"No," I say sternly. "I'm done for today."

Brooklyn pouts. "You're going to let me drink alone?"

I just cross my arms over my chest and stare at her in silence.

"Fine," she says. "I'll make you a deal: have a drink

with me, and I'll let you pay the stupid check. But I won fair and square."

The waitress looks at us like we're insane.

"I'll only agree if I get a rematch," I say. "Using real tiles and words that regular people would know."

"You've got yourself a deal," Brooklyn says. "Provided we can play by *my* rules."

I tell the waitress to bring me another drink, and we work out said rules, which boil down to earning extra points for longer words.

"Fine," I say. "Long words, but normal ones."

"Deal," she says.

The waitress comes back carrying my drink. I suppress a hiccup and turn to her. "Do you have Scrabble tiles?"

No, *now* she looks at us like we're insane. "No," she says, sounding a lot more polite than she looks. "But we might have an old newspaper, with a crossword puzzle."

Brooklyn claps her hands excitedly. "Please bring it."

The waitress arches an eyebrow. "No problem. Anything else?"

"Yeah. Some flour," Brooklyn says.

Flour? Why would she need that for a crossword puzzle?

"Anything else?" The waitress looks at me as if asking, "Do I need to call 911?"

"Yeah," Brooklyn says. "A bowl, please, and more water."

The waitress scurries away before the requests can get weirder, and I stare at Brooklyn expectantly, but she just sits there with a mysterious smile on her beautiful face.

When all the items come out, Brooklyn puts the flour into the bowl, adds water, and mixes it all with her fork.

"What are you making?" I can't help but ask. And why is it making me think of sperm?

Ignoring me, Brooklyn waves for the waitress again.

"Yes?" The waitress isn't hiding her attitude now.

"Do you have a balloon?" Brooklyn asks.

Is this what alcohol poisoning looks like?

The waitress shakes her head.

"What about a condom?" Brooklyn asks.

Curiosity getting the better of me, I take out my wallet and hand the waitress a big tip. "Please," I add. "I'm curious to see where this is going."

Snatching the cash, the waitress leaves and returns with a whole box of condoms. "They have more in the machine in the bathroom," she says. "In case you run out." With that, she leaves us.

Biting her lip, Brooklyn rips a piece of newspaper and dips it into the bowl. And I don't know if it's the condoms or the lip biting, but I'd pay a million dollars for us to be in my bedroom right now.

Oh.

Wait.

She unwraps a condom and starts blowing into it. I get uncomfortably hard.

Soon, the condom is a bulbous balloon shape.

Okay...

I do my best to pretend to be chill.

Brooklyn takes the newspaper piece and wraps it around the blown-up condom. She then prepares another piece and wraps it at a different angle, then does it again and again until the whole thing resembles some sort of mummified whale cock.

"Now we wait for it to dry," she says as I gape at it.

"And then?" I prod.

"And then I paint your face on it," she explains.

I tear my gaze away from the weirdness to look at her quizzically. "Why?"

"Because it's you. A papier-mâché version."

That's what I thought this thing might be—papier-mâché, not me. Brooklyn mentioned that this art form was her version of surfing.

"It's already like looking in the mirror," I say, tilting my gaze back to the cock mummy. "Are you sure you need the paint?"

She downs her drink. "I'm sure." She balls up a little bit of the newspaper, rolls it into a tight ball, and adds what I'm guessing is an ear to "my" head.

I wonder what her alcohol tolerance is?

As I ponder that, she pulls out her lipstick and draws lips on "my" newspaper face. Looking pleased, she searches for the waitress.

Nope. Wasn't faking. Before she can ask the waitress for any more alcohol, I gesture for the check and ask Brooklyn, "Would you like to take that stroll across the Bridge of Lions?"

Her eyes glint excitedly. "That one near the castle?"

I check the time. "You know, if we hurry, we could get a quick look inside the castle before our stroll."

She grabs her artwork and leaps to her feet, swaying a bit. "Let's do it."

"One second." I wait until the waitress brings the check and then toss the required amount of cash on the table, plus another tip. "*Now* we can go."

When I stand up, I realize that Brooklyn isn't the only one who might've overindulged. I don't think the restaurant is usually spinning the way it is now, nor do my legs usually feel like cotton candy.

"Here." I offer Brooklyn my elbow. "If we're going to stroll, we might as well do it properly."

Also, the chances of us falling go down if we're inter-connected—at least I hope so.

Without hesitation, Brooklyn slides her tiny hand into the crook of my elbow, and her touch sends a zing of lust right into my dick.

Just perfect. Walking is going to be even harder now —pun intended.

———

"This is the last time I drink St. Augustine vodka," I mutter to no one in particular after a few blocks. "And I mean it... this time."

Brooklyn hiccups. "You've made this oath before?"

"Only once or twice." We cross the road, walking reasonably straight... I think.

"Wow," Brooklyn says. "It all looks even better from here."

I follow her gaze. The Intracoastal does look picturesque, but I think it has more to do with the gorgeous colors of the setting sun.

"Let's hurry. It's even better from the castle parapet." I pick up the pace, but despite my best efforts, we don't make it.

"I'm sorry. We're already closed," the guy in the booth says when we arrive.

The expression on Brooklyn's face is unacceptable, so I dig into my wallet and slip the guy a few bills as stealthily as I can. "Do you think you could make an exception, just this once?"

"Fine." The guy pockets the money and leaves his booth. "If anyone asks, you're good friends of mine."

Brooklyn places "my" papier-mâché face on the booth counter. "Is it okay if I leave Evan here?"

The ticket guy looks at me askance.

"It's fine," I say. "Better your hands be free."

Brooklyn blows an air kiss to the condom-based Evan, then joins me in following our reluctant guide.

Once we're inside the castle, the ticket guy leaves and I lead Brooklyn into the courtyard. She oohs and aahs at everything, which inspires me to recall some of the useless factoids I learned from the countless tours of this place my classmates and I took back in high school—like the fact that it's made from coquina.

"Co-quinoa?" Brooklyn repeats. "Is that a companion of a seed masquerading as a grain?"

I grin loopily. "It's a soft limestone composed of shells and coral."

"Why make the castle out of that?"

"It makes the walls resistant to cannon fire."

"Right," she says with an eyeroll. "Because as every hermit crab knows, sturdy seashells are as strong as Kevlar."

I shrug. "I'm just telling you what they told us during the tours. I'm not exactly a military engineer."

She opens her mouth to say something else, but the view of the sunset from the parapet catches her attention. She stares at it, open-mouthed—as I stare at her instead. She has a classically beautiful nose, slightly-rosy-from-excitement cheeks, and—

Fuck, she catches me ogling and moistens her lips.

Double fuck. I'm getting pulled toward those lips, like a pirate toward booty. And now I'm thinking about Brooklyn's nice, round booty—like my hard-on wasn't obvious already. I bend my head, unable to help myself, and whatever force is working on me seems to impact her as well because she tips her head back, her gaze locked on mine.

Our lips crash, and all pirate-ship and cannonball-related metaphors flee my mind. Brooklyn tastes like green tea ice cream and smells like yuzu and cloves—a head-spinning combination that makes me want to quadruple the million dollars I'm willing to give up to magically end up in bed with her. Maybe I'd even sextuple that amount... emphasis on the first three letters of that word, of course.

My hands slide into her silky hair as I sweep my tongue deeper into the soft recesses of her mouth, feeling her soft body molding against mine—

Some asshole clears his throat. "We're officially closed."

Fuck. Brooklyn and I spring apart, and I have to take deep breaths to control violent urges toward the interrupter.

"I'm sorry," says the guy I bribed earlier. "We have to close up."

Looking somewhat confused, Brooklyn touches her kiss-swollen lips, making me crave them all over again. "Look at those lights on the boardwalk," she says, apropos of nothing.

"Yeah. Gorgeous." With a monumental effort, I drag my eyes away from Brooklyn's face and take another deep breath.

"To the Bridge of Lions!" Brooklyn grabs my hand.

Seriously? I don't know how many more zings my poor balls can take before they turn turquoise.

Hands clasped, we get back downstairs, but before leaving, Brooklyn takes a few selfies of the two of us, then asks the guy kicking us out to take a pic from a distance.

Damn. This is progressing suspiciously like a date—with a kiss and everything.

This is when it really hits me. We kissed. A part of me still can't believe it. And it was the most amazing kiss ever. Unless... is the vodka making me think so? Beer goggles are a thing, so maybe—

"Almost forgot," Brooklyn says, grabbing her artwork as we pass by the ticket booth.

Does this mean she's sobering up, or is it the opposite?

The feeling of this being a date strengthens as we stroll hand in hand, chatting about everything and nothing. I tell her what I like about surfing, she tells me why she loves to work with animals—and that she wants to do more of it in the future, preferably by becoming a vet.

"I could totally see you as a vet," I say. "You should do it."

Her smile falters. "Maybe one day."

Ah. Right. She's on vacation, and I'm reminding her about work and responsibilities.

Speaking of reminders, she's here merely on vacation. Until now, the haze of alcohol had made me forget that and the fact that I'm not very datable.

As if on cue, the lights on the boardwalk and the bridge ahead of us come on, creating an extremely romantic atmosphere.

Fuck me.

Brooklyn waves at the merry people on a passing boat, and I use that moment to instruct Boone to meet us on the other side of the bridge. I also tell him that I'm going to pay electronically, so we can avoid discussing money in front of Brooklyn.

"Would you want to go on a boat ride tomorrow?" I ask after I put my phone away.

She gapes at me. "You have a boat?"

"No." Not yet anyway, but purchasing one is on my

to-do list. "My dad has one, and I can borrow it anytime."

She looks wistful. "You and your dad are close?"

I nod. "When my mother passed, he didn't take it well, so for a short time, it almost felt like I was the dad and he the kid, but now it's all back to normal. He takes me fishing and gives me unsolicited life advice."

Brooklyn's wistful look turns downright dejected. "I haven't spoken to my father—or mother—in seven years."

Oh, fuck. "I'm sorry. I didn't realize."

Her eyes glint. "It's not your fault. It's theirs. Their love was conditional, and as soon as I did something to displease them, it was withdrawn."

What the fuck? What kind of parents are those? She's better off without them if that's how they are. Tamping down the surge of anger on her behalf, I squeeze her hand. "It's their loss."

She gives me a weak smile and points across the street with her free hand. "Can we get another drink there?"

Curse this area and its million and one bars. We really shouldn't imbibe anymore, but given what she's just told me, I can't refuse.

"I'm buying," she warns me.

"Fine," I grumble. "But just one drink."

"Or its equal volume in shots," she says.

Before I can voice my opinion, she drags me to the bar and, once inside, orders four shots "as a start."

I down three of the four shots, mostly to make sure she doesn't get alcohol poisoning. After she orders four more, I drink three again, and then I sneak the bartender an extra-large tip and whisper-beg that she not take any more orders from Brooklyn.

I haven't had this much to drink since my college days.

"Did you pay her?" Brooklyn demands. "We agreed that I'd pay."

"He tipped me," the bartender tells her and winks at me. "Which means you still owe me twenty bucks."

Brooklyn hands over the cash, then grabs her artwork and my hand before we resume the epic journey to the Bridge of Lions.

"Do you think men and women can be friends?" Brooklyn asks out of nowhere, just as we step on said bridge.

Is this about the kiss? Is she preparing to tell me she wants me in the friend zone? Unless... "Is that a *When Harry met Sally* reference?"

She squeezes my hand teasingly. "Perhaps."

"Well, what do *you* think?"

She shrugs. "My besties are both women, but I think, in theory at least, it's possible."

"If we're talking platonic friends, I think I could be that with *some* women," I say. "But if I find a woman extremely attractive, being just friends would be difficult." Like in *this* case. Then again, she won't be in Florida long enough to need me even as a friend.

"Yeah. I think if I found the guy attractive, I'd have trouble with platonic-ness too."

My lips quirk. "I don't think 'platonic-ness' is a word, but if it were, it would be sixteen points."

"Are you angling for that Scrabble rematch?"

I narrow my eyes at her. "I don't need to angle. You agreed. A deal is a deal."

"Why are you so eager to lose again?" She takes a selfie with papier-mâché Evan.

"I won't lose." At least I hope not.

"Is that Boone?" Brooklyn asks, pointing at a beat-up Oldsmobile Aurora pulling up to the curb.

"Yep." And I hope that car survives the trip home.

The good news is that Bonnie is with Boone, which means I have no choice but to sit next to Brooklyn in the back. To that end, I get the door for her.

"Thank you." She bats her long eyelashes at me before climbing inside. "It will be a shame to defeat such a gentleman."

"What are you defeating him in, hon?" Bonnie asks with her signature drawl.

"Scrabble," Brooklyn answers.

"Oh. Boone and I have been fixin' to play that game," Bonnie says and flashes the gap where she recently lost a tooth in an attempt to milk one of Calvin's pet cows.

"How about we play using the app?" I suggest.

Bonnie is excited, but Brooklyn seems dubious.

As soon as we start playing, I regret it. The screen is blurry, and looking at the app is making me carsick. At least that's my story—a big, strong guy like me wouldn't feel woozy from a little alcohol. No way.

By the time we enter my community, Bonnie has

beaten us both and claps her hands in glee. "Well, I do declare. Did y'all think just because I'm this hot, I'm stupid?"

"I'm not sure about Brooklyn," I say. "But I think we'll have to have a rematch when everyone involved is sober." And I'm not admitting that I'm not.

"You never accept a loss, do you?" Is it the alcohol, or does Brooklyn always have that much snark in her tone? "Speaking of, if Bonnie hadn't won, I would have."

"That's not true," I say, though I wouldn't bet my life on it.

"I reckon no man likes it when his woman beats him at something," Bonnie says. "At least, Boone don't like it when I do it to him."

Should I tell her Brooklyn isn't my woman? Also, why isn't Brooklyn herself issuing the correction?

"You never win at anything," Boone grumps.

"Is that right?" Bonnie turns toward her husband. "Was it you who predicted last month's NASCAR race?"

"You got lucky."

Bonnie's eyes turn into slits. "What about the one before that?"

"The winning driver was your cousin," Boone says—and, thankfully, he turns onto my driveway.

As Brooklyn and I leave the car, Boone and Bonnie get into one of their famous screaming matches.

"I guess this is me." Brooklyn nods at her rental.

"Sure," I say. "Unless… we play that game you owe me."

Brooklyn's eyes glint excitedly. "You're on."

We rush inside and I set everything up on the kitchen table as Brooklyn goes to "powder her nose," whatever that means.

Harry clickety-clacks up to me and sticks his wet nose into my leg.

Human dude. You're back. Some munchies would be greatly appreciated.

As I get the food ready for Harry, Sally rubs herself on my leg.

Our evil captor should know, we escaped this horrible palace earlier today, but then returned, in case tonight is the night that the tomcat-in-shining-armor rescues us—and vivisects you.

I give Sally her food too, then turn and see that Brooklyn is already sitting at the table.

"Care to make your rematch more interesting?" she asks.

I arch an eyebrow. "What did you have in mind?"

"Two words." Brooklyn hiccups. "Strip Scrabble."

Chapter Thirteen

BROOKLYN

Evan's blue-green gaze is the ocean before a storm. "You're on."

Does he mean 'turned on?' If so, how did he guess that I am? In my defense, our not-date was so hot even a nun would need new panties at this point... unless they don't wear any.

"A piece of clothing per game?" Evan asks. "Or when we reach a certain score?"

"Both," I say. "But let's play with extra tiles so we can make longer words. Also, let's put a time limit on the game—whoever has the highest score when the timer goes off wins."

"Anything else?"

I throw a few more rules at him until the game is almost exactly like how I usually play it—but I don't tell him this part. If there were such a thing as a Scrabble lawyer, I'd make a good one. Oh, and this gives me an idea: I should look for a way to use the word "jurispru-dential" in this game, if I get the chance.

"Okay." He fishes a tile from inside the tile bag and then offers the bag to me.

I get an E to his A, so he is the first to go.

Grr. I can't wait until he's got less clothes on.

When I get my tiles, I sort them from A to Z as I always do. And score! I got a blank tile too. Maybe I'll finally be able to form the word 'alphabetization'—I've always wanted to do that.

As we begin, sadly, a chance to play 'alphabetization' doesn't turn up, but I have an even better word: 'psycho-analyzing.'

"Nice." Making a big show out of it, Evan slides off his shoe.

Crap. He's wearing socks.

"Coward." I glance at his pants.

If I were sober enough to psychoanalyze myself, I'd ponder why I'm so eager for another high score. Is this objectification of Evan? Oh, hey, 'objectification' would be a great word to use—if only I could find the letters. Either way, I get lucky again and score hugely with 'mischaracterize.'

Evan slides off his other shoe with relish.

Is he happy to be losing? If so, I've mischaracterized him.

We resume playing, and Evan somehow gets a word that I've never seen used in the game: 'ventriloquizing.'

I narrow my eyes. "Is that even a legal word?"

Evan points at his dog. "Dude, dudette, you should

raise the stakes and play for peanut butter. Or butt sniffs." He locks eyes with me. "What I just did was ventriloquizing."

"Fine." Copying his earlier show, I take off my shoe. I do a decent job of shoe-shedding, I think, because he looks at my bare foot with such hunger you'd think it were a naked boob.

We play head-to-head for a while until I get him with my favorite word thus far: 'demythologizing.'

Now we're talking. Evan takes off his sock, exposing a strong, manly foot.

Hmm. Who told me they find men's feet hideous— Jolene or Dorothy? Either way, Evan's sexy foot is actively demythologizing that claim as we speak.

I wonder, is it safe to ride a foot, sexually? Or would that lead to an itchy vag? Asking for a friend.

Utilizing some cat ninja skills, Sally appears on the table in front of me and stares me down. Crap. Between this and all the foot musings, I've accidentally set up Evan for 'hypnotizability.' Maybe I have a strong hypnotizability, and the cat is using it against me to assist her owner.

Either way, I take off my other shoe.

Evan's eyes gleam as he stares at it.

Can two people develop a foot fetish out of nowhere? Maybe via the likes of *T. gondii*, the cat parasite, except a different one that transmits itself when you lick (or ride) someone's feet? Maybe it first lived on the foot of a bigfoot?

Wait.

I look at my tiles and at the board.

Score! I play 'cryptozoologist.'

Evan arches an eyebrow. "What's that?"

I lift my chin. "A person who searches for cryptids, which are creatures like the yeti and the Loch Ness Monster."

Evan undoes the top button of his shirt. "Sure, it is."

By all the yetis... Evan slowly and teasingly undoes the next button and the one below that.

I fight the urge to rip the shirt off his body because that's not very lady-like. After what feels like an hour of hormonal torture, he takes the shirt off and drops it on the floor.

Wow. I've seen him shirtless before, but it's like he's gotten hotter, and somehow even more ripped. Also, is it the alcohol in my system, or does Evan's sixpack somehow have ten sections—each begging me to lick it? At least the number of pecs is still two, as expected, but they look steelier than before, more defined. Even his nipples are—

"Take a picture," Evan says with a smirk. "It might last longer."

Ah. Right. I'm ogling him. The picture idea isn't a bad one, but I chicken out. "Let's just keep playing."

The next word I play is 'ache.' Soon after it's 'ardor,' with 'need' after that, followed by 'heat.'

Evan's eyes gleam as his lips twitch in a cocky grin. "Am I detecting a pattern?"

Fuck. I was just about to make 'thirst,' but now I can't. 'Pang?' No, still follows the theme he's mocking.

With a sigh, I play 'fungi,' which seems safe—except Evan slaughters me with 'governmentalize.'

I give him a narrowed-eye stare. "You threw me off my game on purpose."

He grins. "Are you welching?"

I huff. "No way." Then again, all I have on is my dress with a bra and panties underneath.

His grin goes away. "It's okay if you want to stop."

I scoff. "And admit defeat?"

He gestures at the score paper. "You're actually still in the lead."

"No." If I stop now, I won't feel like I've won. I'm bizarrely curious how Evan will react when my dress comes off, though I'm also quite a bit anxious.

The curiosity wins, and I stand up, albeit a bit unsteady on my feet.

Evan opens his mouth, but no words emerge.

Pulse racing, I slide the right strap of my dress off my shoulder.

Evan is a statue in his chair. Only his eyes reflect the storm going on inside.

I slip off the other strap.

Is his jaw ticking?

Feeling bolder, I mime his slow disrobing as I wriggle out of the dress, and by the time I'm done, Evan's gaze is ravenous, like a wolf staring at a gazelle.

My skin tingles, my face burns, and my heart pounds so fast I feel hot and cold. What am I doing? Then again, I feel oddly good too, powerful in a strange way.

Is this why strippers do what they do? Because it's

such a rush? Then again, it wouldn't be nearly as exciting —or exciting at all, really—if it were anyone but Evan devouring me with his eyes.

I swallow hard and sit back at the table, like nothing's the matter.

"You sure you want to keep playing?" Evan asks, his voice hoarse.

Great question. One more loss, and I have to decide between my bra and panties, a tough choice. But screw it. The stripper in me is up for either. "Are you sure *you* want to keep playing?" I manage to ask sultrily.

At least I think it's sultrily. Could also be with a slight slur.

In reply, Evan grabs a handful of tiles from the bag.

All right. We're doing this.

My panties feel damp. They might be the item of clothing to go next—for reasons.

We both play a few short words, but then he gets a long one—but not so long that I have to strip.

Then I spot it and almost shout in glee. Another winner for me: 'recognizability.'

"Good one," Evan says, and it clearly costs him.

"You want to welch?" I ask, parroting his earlier tone.

With a slight eyeroll, he stands up.

Holy objectification. He slowly unzips his pants.

Swaying his hips as though he's an extra on *Magic Mike*, he drags his pants down.

Am I about to keel over?

Nope. I'm still upright when the pants are gone, so I'm very aware of the bulge in Evan's boxers. A huge bulge. Longer and harder than any of the words we've played thus far.

When he sits back down, the table blocks the bulge from my view, allowing me to think straight.

"You sure you want to keep playing?" I ask, my voice more than a little husky.

He nods.

All right. Unless he's wearing a cock ring under those boxers, he's only got one item of clothing left, while I have two. Side note: is a cock ring even an item of clothing? It seems more like jewelry to me. Or an accessory, like glasses.

Evan plays his next word, 'craze.'

Hmm.

Then: 'fervor.'

Wait a second.

When he plays 'hots,' I call it official. "You're following the same theme that I did."

He shrugs.

Brows furrowing, I put my own word on the board, a very unsexy 'crud.'

Evan's eyes gleam with triumph. "Fine. I'll break the pattern."

Oh, no.

Yep.

He puts the word 'exchangeability' on the board.

Shit. Exchangeability is something that bras and panties do not have.

My heartbeat speeds up.

I know I said I'd keep playing, but this is serious—

and I have no idea what to take off. Losing panties would usually be worse, but since we're playing sitting down, Evan wouldn't be staring at my bits the whole next round, the way he would if my breasts were bare.

"Look, Brooklyn," Evan says in a serious tone. "You don't have to do anything you're not okay with."

"Nice try." If I were still feeling as bold as before, I'd stand up, turn back to him, bend down, and then slide down my panties—maybe twerking the whole time.

Turns out I don't have that in me, even though my mind is more than a little fuzzy from all the drinks. Instead, I slide my panties down under the cover of the table like a coward and cross my legs. Hopefully, I won't leave a damp spot on the seat this way.

Evan stares at me pointedly.

Oh, right, he has no idea what I've done.

Flushing, I raise my hand and wave my panties like a slutty white flag.

"Fucking fuck," Evan grunts.

Does that mean he likes this? Or has he not seen lace before? It's possible the women he's dated have never bothered wearing any panties.

With faux calm, I grab more tiles and resume the game, praying he's unfocused enough to give me an edge.

Grr. I'm not sure if Evan is trying to mess with my head or what, but the words he plays include things like 'cup,' 'coax,' 'nip,' and the least subtle of all, 'lick.'

My nipples, which thank goodness are still covered by my bra, are rock hard.

Ignoring my body's stupid reactions, I play random words, bide my time, and focus.

Is that...?

Yes, it is.

Whooping with glee, I spell out the last word of our game on the table: 'theatricalizing.' Then I look up at Evan, smirking. "Look... You don't have to do anything you're not okay with."

Brushing off my words, he stands up, exposing the bulge once more.

Oh, my.

He grabs his boxers. "You can turn away if this is too much."

"Yeah. Not going to happen. I earned this show."

"Okay." He tugs his boxers down, foregoing a stripper routine.

When his cock juts out from its prison, my eyes boggle and I catch myself clutching my chest, as if I had pearls there.

The thing is gorgeous. The words 'big' or 'thick' or 'long' don't do it justice. A longer word is required. Something adopted from German perhaps. Something that would win at Scrabble any day of the week. To put this in Jolene's terms, this is like that giant dose of vitamin D that your doctor gives you when your blood test shows a deficiency.

"So," says the guy attached to Vitamin D. "As the winner, what do you want?"

Forcing myself to lift my gaze, I clear my parched throat. "What do you mean?"

"We never talked about the prize for winning this game," he says. "Doesn't it feel like there should be one?"

I swallow hard as sweat trickles down my spine. "What do you have in mind?"

Evan's eyes gleam, and Vitamin D twitches—no doubt creating a gust of wind. "Anything you want."

What do I want? And why am I getting to my feet? Wait, why am I walking toward him? Better yet, where is my hand going? Because it's reaching for Vitamin D like it hasn't seen sunlight in decades.

"Fuck," Evan grunts when my hand reaches its destination. "That's a great choice."

Vitamin D feels hard and velvety in my hand. "We shouldn't do this."

"Not when drunk," Evan says. "And not with you leaving so soon."

I stroke Vitamin D up and down its length. "I'm glad we're on the same page." With that, I rise on tiptoes and slant my lips over his.

Chapter Fourteen

EVAN

This feels amazing. Her lips are soft and pliant, and as to her small hand on my cock—I have no words.

She pulls away, releases my dick—unfortunately—and then bends down, very fortunately giving me a majestic view of her ass, with just a hint of pink pussy.

I didn't think I could get harder, but what do you know? All I want now is to bury my face in there, then lick and suck until she screams my name in—

Wait. What is she looking for down in the pile of clothes?

Ah. Right. She takes out one of the condoms she got from the waitress, originally for her papier-mâché masterpiece.

"I'm clean," she murmurs, looking up at me.

"So am I." And with the vasectomy, I can't get her pregnant, but I don't want to get into that right now, so I'll just use a condom anyway.

"Good to know." She kneels on top of the pile of our clothes. "That means I can do this."

Hold up—

Fuuuck. She looks me in the eyes as she puts the tip of my cock in her mouth.

Since words are difficult, I make some sort of cave-man-like guttural sound to show my appreciation.

She slides me in deeper.

My balls tighten.

She gives me a sensual lick and cups said balls.

I almost fall backward, in part from the pleasure, but maybe also from the alcohol buzz. "Let's take this to the bedroom," I manage to say after I stabilize myself.

She frees her mouth, her lips glistening. "That's a great idea."

All right. I grab her as if I were a fireman and my house were about to burn down.

She squeals good-naturedly as I sprint to the bed, but she quiets down as I lay her on the blanket and admire the view.

Fuck. This has been the beginning of almost all my wet dreams as of late, and now it's happening for real.

I lock eyes with her. My voice is a low, thick growl. "I want to see you."

She spreads her legs, revealing the majestic pussy I got a glimpse of earlier.

My cock turns almost painfully hard. "I meant 'lose the bra,' but this is even better."

Blushing fiercely, she unhooks her bra, revealing perky breasts with nipples as pink as her pussy.

"You're stunning," I say solemnly and still feel like I'm understating.

"Thank you," she breathes. "You're not so bad yourself."

I've heard compliments from women before, but I've never felt as good from one as I do now. Smirking, I join her on the bed and teasingly kiss her upper thigh.

Her skin breaks in gooseflesh.

Smiling into her flesh, I place a kiss half an inch higher.

She tenses.

I take pity on her and close the distance to her pussy, where I lap at her folds the way I've been dying to for what feels like forever.

Her silky flesh tastes divine and is deliciously warm under my tongue. I could spend hours here, relishing this.

A moan escapes her lips.

I slide my tongue very gently over her perfect little bud of a clit.

Another moan is my reward.

"Good girl," I murmur without moving my mouth away, and she clearly likes the feeling of my lips vibrating as I speak because she arches her back and grabs my hair, urging me on.

I'm happy to oblige and speed up my tongue's ministrations.

Her grip on my hair strengthens, though not enough to hurt.

"Come for me," I croon, purposefully creating more vibrations.

I'm not sure if it's my words or the command, but she scream-moans and thrashes on the bed while under my tongue. Her pussy spasms and twitches, driving me crazy with lust.

I sound barely coherent as I move over her, rasping, "I want to be inside you."

It's what I've been craving, and I can't believe it's about to happen.

"Yes, please," she gasps.

Claiming her lips in an animalistic kiss, I finally enter her.

Chapter Fifteen

BROOKLYN

O h, my.

Tasting myself on Evan's breath is the hottest thing that has happened to me in seven years. Actually, coming from his tongue was.

Wait, no. The honor belongs to the moment when Vitamin D makes its grand entrance. Or more specifically, enters me. It's so big that my muscles have to stretch to adjust for it, but once they do, the feeling of fullness—and rightness—is frighteningly good.

It's like I've suddenly become whole.

Evan thrusts into me, gently.

Wow.

He does it again, still carefully.

Grr. Judging by how ravenous his kiss is, he's restraining himself. So I grab his butt—which is hard-muscled perfection—and ram him into me.

He takes my not-so-subtle hint. Oh, my, does he ever. He pistons into me harder, faster, his movements borderline savage, and I feel a new orgasm coiling inside me. Every muscle in my body tenses, and tingles of delight run up and down my spine as white flecks dot my vision.

Evan shifts his kisses to my neck as he impossibly speeds up his thrusts.

My entire body is covered in goosebumps of need, and my hands grab his ass again, without any ulterior motive this time, just to have something to hold on to.

Fucking me harder, he sucks on my earlobe as if it were a clit.

I cry out, my nails digging into his ass.

Evan's eyes, hazy with lust, meet mine, and I tumble over the explosive edge.

Yes.

Yes.

Yes!

With a loud scream and my insides quivering all over Vitamin D, I come so hard the white flecks in my vision go supernova and every nerve ending in my body sizzles with electric ecstasy.

Above me, Evan groans in pleasure, grinding into me as he reaches his release.

———

The aftermath is as soft and foggy as the sex was wild. Holding me like a little spoon, Evan strokes me all over as I catch my breath. I feel both ridiculously happy and wrung out, so I yawn. Loudly.

Evan chuckles into my hair. "Did my performance bore you that much?"

Since he already sounds cocky, I don't tell him I have a case of the proverbial fucked-out brains—or that his performance was the best I've ever experienced, by a wide margin. Instead, I yawn again. "You did well. Especially considering it was our first time."

"I don't like the sound of that," he says. "I think you owe me another rematch."

He wants to do that whole thing again? With me? The thought fills me with languid hope and contentedness as I fall asleep.

———

I wake up because my phone has somehow turned into a jackhammer, and its hellish vibrations are drilling a hole in my skull.

I check what the infernal device wants.

Oh. It's a video call from Jolene and Dorothy. I think I know two people by those names, but I don't want to talk to them right now. Or talk at all.

I mean to dismiss the call, but I accidentally click "accept"—the dexterity of my fingers is clearly compromised.

"You slut," Jolene says instead of a hello. "You totally got some last night."

Is Jolene like that boy in *The Sixth Sense*, but in her case, she sees freshly fucked people?

Speaking of freshly fucked, it's all coming back to me now. Drinks. Strip Scrabble. Vitamin D overdose.

Blood leaving my face, I turn to see if the owner of Vitamin D has heard what Jolene said.

Hmm. Evan is missing from the bed.

Weird. I'm pretty sure this is his house.

"I'll call you back," I say in a hoarse voice. "Oh, and please, for the love of all the vacation gods, do *not* call me at the crack of dawn."

"Actually, it's noon," Dorothy says defensively just as I hang up on them.

Noon? I immediately think of Reagan and start dialing the camp. Once I hear his cheerful and excited voice on the other end, I breathe a sigh of relief and wish him a good day, careful not to do so too loudly.

After we say our goodbyes, I check my Octothorpe Glorp, half expecting my blood alcohol content to conveniently appear on the screen.

My dear Precious, if I could dream, I'd dream about being a phlebotomist so that I could have access to the healing elixir that is your life's blood. I'd gladly inform you of BAC, or infections, or unwanted pregnancies, or if your blood tastes bad. Alas, the elixir is not accessible to me... at least outside of my fantasies.

Hmm. Where is Evan?

"Evan?" I shout, but it comes out like a husky whisper.

I walk up to the bathroom and knock.

No reply.

I pull the door open.

The room is empty.

Maybe this is a blessing in disguise? I'm probably not in any condition to be seen by Evan, or anyone else at the moment.

Entering the bathroom, I spot a sealed toothbrush that someone has left for me.

Okay. Seems like Evan was here at some point in the recent past and thought of me.

That's nice, but where is he now?

After brushing my teeth and washing my face, I feel awake enough to tackle the elephant in the room: I slept with Evan.

More accurately, we went on what amounts to a date, and then he gave me multiple orgasms.

And I liked it all. And want to do it again. Badly. Ideally, while I'm sober so I can remember every little detail.

No. That's crazy talk. I'm still only here on vacation, so at most, Evan and I can have a fling, which until last night, I didn't think I'd ever want.

But... didn't we just have a fling? Or is it a one-night stand at this point? Is there a difference?

Either way, what harm would it do to fling my pussy at him some more?

I look at myself in the mirror sternly. The harm could be immeasurable because days like yesterday could lead to feelings.

And maybe already have.

No. Can't allow feelings. Even if by some magic, I were to turn into a Florida native and therefore no longer hold the status of a tourist, I still haven't told Evan about Reagan—the most important part of my life. But if I tell Evan that I have a child—one of those creatures that he hates—he'll run for the hills, assuming he's not already hiding in said hills.

Speaking of that, I come out of the bedroom and search the house.

All I find is Sally, who narrows her eyes at me in the clear feline equivalent of slut shaming.

"Where is your human?" I ask.

No reply.

"Evan?"

No one answers.

Wow. Is it possible he did the classic one-night-stand thing and slinked away? But can you do that when the one-night stand was in your own house?

Maybe. Could he be watching me through some security camera, waiting until I get a clue and leave? Then again, I'll still be his renter for a while, so avoiding me might be tricky.

Hmm. Jokes aside, could last night have meant so little to him? He said he wasn't into flings, but he did drink, and he does own a penis, so...

My phone rings again.

Is it Evan?

No. It's my friends.

Maybe *they* can shed some light on this?

I accept the call but tell them to hold on.

Walking over to the fridge, I take out milk, locate cereal in the pantry, and make myself some breakfast. If he truly is waiting for me to leave, I'm not going to make it easy for him. Besides, breakfast might absorb some of the alcohol still sloshing through my veins.

"Spill already," Jolene says when I finally return to my phone.

"Yeah," Dorothy chimes in. I can only see the top of her face on the screen, but she seems very curious because her eyebrows are raised, and her forehead is wrinkled.

"One second." I take my breakfast to the porch, assuming that even if Evan is spying on me, he's unlikely to overhear me outside. "It all started when Evan brought over a treasure map," I say, and proceed to tell them everything.

"I'm so proud," Jolene interrupts when I get to the bedroom part. "Is this how you feel when Reagan brings home an A?"

"Yeah. Those are exactly the same situations," I say with an eyeroll. But I do wonder: would Evan give me an A for last night?

"Please continue," Dorothy says, her voice not quite her own.

"Hey, not cool," Jolene says. "You can't masturbate when your girlfriend is dishing, no matter how sexy the story."

Dorothy gets so close to her phone that we can only see one pantomiming eyebrow. "Unlike some, I don't masturbate twenty times a day."

"Who does?" Jolene makes a show of looking around, like secret masturbators might be hiding in her kitchen. "From my experience, after about ten sessions, soreness becomes a real issue, so whoever the twenty-times woman is, I'd like to ask her to give me some tips."

"You know what, I'm done." I move my finger to end the call.

"No!" they both shout in unison.

"I'm sorry," Jolene says.

"Same," Dorothy adds.

Fine. I finish my story, going into graphic detail in the process. Unfortunately, reliving it all makes me hot and bothered, and wishing for a lot more. Soon.

"But when I woke up, he wasn't here," I say in conclusion. "And I have no idea what it means."

"Did he leave you a note?" Dorothy asks.

"Or text?" Jolene adds.

I examine my phone.

No texts.

I haven't looked for a note, though. "Hold on," I say and retrace my steps through the house. No notes in the kitchen, but when I return to the bedroom and glance at the nightstand, I feel like an idiot because there it is, next to the papier-mâché Evan.

A note written in masculine handwriting.

"What does it say?" Jolene demands.

Great question.

Hands trembling, I reach for the note.

Chapter Sixteen

EVAN

Earlier

Despite the throbbing in my temples, I somehow manage to finish my surfing lesson, all the while hoping the kids can't smell the vodka fumes on my breath.

Like with my Airbnb business, I do this volunteering gig as a way to socialize and stay down to earth, but today, thanks to a killer hangover, I wonder if I should've hired someone to cover for me.

But no. What if the guy I hired was some sicko? Not that the camp's administration would let me do that anyway. Regardless of how much money I've donated to this place, their first concern is the safety of the campers.

As all the kids run off to their next activity, Reagan stays behind.

Harry sniffs Reagan like an old friend. The kid takes out a peanut butter and jelly sandwich from his pocket and shares it, winning major brownie points with both me and the dog.

I wonder what he wants this time. Has he sprouted hair in another location?

"Hi, Mr. Evan," he says shyly.

I smile reassuringly at him, and somehow that makes my headache recede. A little.

"Hey, bud. Call me Evan."

"Sorry... Evan," Reagan says. "Can I ask you a question?"

"Sure." I gulp some water from my bottle in the hopes of alleviating the worst of the hangover.

Reagan shifts from foot to foot, clearly unsure if he should ask whatever it is.

Seriously? What could it be? Chest hair? Mine didn't come in until I was in my late twenties, but maybe—

"What's anal?" he finally blurts.

The water goes up my nose, and I have to cough to regain my composure.

It's official. I'm not going to drink liquids around this kid ever again.

"What a fascinating question," I say when I can speak. To buy myself more time, I cap the water bottle. "What's the context?"

Please don't say porn or—

"Con—what?" Reagan asks.

"Context. As in, where did you hear it? In what sentence? Under what circumstances?"

"Ah. One of the counselors said it to the other," Reagan says.

My hands ball into fists. "What did he say?" If I learn that someone has been having inappropriate conversations around the children, I'm going to—

"*She* said 'Yes, I checked it twice, Brian. Stop being so anal,'" Reagan says in an imitation of a teen girl's voice.

Oh. My hands unclench, and I exhale in relief before asking, "Do you know what persnickety means?"

Reagan cocks his head. "Fussy?"

Despite not knowing what "anal" or "context" is, the kid clearly has a great vocabulary. "She meant something like that, but with a compulsive component."

He looks less sure. "Like you have to be fussy?"

"Kind of. There's usually an obsessive element to it as well. Like when someone likes neatness so much they force others to be neat, or they like correct spelling and grammar so much they correct them for other people."

"Hmm," Reagan says. "My mom might be into anal."

It takes an elephantine effort to keep my face impassive. "You don't say 'into' before an adjective."

Reagan grins mischievously. "Are you showing me an example of how to be anal?"

Clever little munchkin. "Exactly."

"Thank you." He grins at me. "I loved your lesson, by the way. When I grow up, I also want to be a surfer."

Huh. He even looks like some of the surfer dudes I know, with his long hair and his unusually chill attitude.

"I'm sure I'll make a surfer out of you before the summer is out," I say.

His smile turns upside down. "I'm not here till the end of the summer. Only five more days."

With that, he runs off, leaving me feeling melancholy for no reason at all.

————

"You look terrible," my father says when I walk into his house with Harry on my heels, wagging his tail. "Those bags under your eyes have bags."

"Thanks." I rub said baggy eyes. "That's why I've come. I want your hangover cure."

After Mom died, Dad drank so much he became quite the expert on hangover cures—that is, until he joined AA.

"Hangover?" Dad's expression turns worried. "What was the occasion?"

It's been a while since he's missed things like birthdays, but the memory must linger, so I can see why he'd be concerned. That or maybe he's worried I'll start to overindulge the way he did.

"I was just keeping someone else company," I say. "And after today, I think I'm going to avoid alcohol for a few years."

Dad grins knowingly. "A female someone?"

"It's not like that. But speaking of her, it's best if you double the cure."

He grabs his blender. "Who is she?"

I sigh. "A tourist."

He wrinkles his nose. "From where?"

"New York," I say and expect the nose wrinkle to worsen.

Dad shrugs instead. "I'm sure she's got ways to compensate for that nearly fatal flaw."

I smile. "She plays Scrabble."

"Well." He dumps half a bag of spinach into the blender. "There you go. That alone means she's a keeper."

Even if she is, I'm not—but I don't go into that with my dad because in his eyes, I can do no wrong.

"Tell me more about her," he says.

"Like what?"

"Oh, don't be like that. How did you meet?"

Fine. As he makes the concoction, I tell him how Brooklyn and I grumped at each other when we first met, and how she almost drowned.

When I'm done, Dad blinks, his eyes suspiciously damp. "It's eerie," he says after a moment. "Your story reminds me so much of how I met your mother."

I frown. "I thought you went to high school together."

"Right, and I spilled chemicals on her when we first met in the lab. She then threw a frog at my face."

"And you saved her life too?"

Dad gives me an exasperated look. "I got her out of the chemical-drenched dress, didn't I? That's despite the frog tossing, mind you. I also gave her my jacket to cover herself."

"You're right. It's the exact same story."

"And that means she's also your soulmate." Dad

sprinkles dried ginger into the blender. "The way your mother was mine."

"I thought you didn't believe in souls," I say.

He gives me a sidelong glance. "The 'soul' is just a word that describes what happens when the computers that are our brains do their computing. Anyway, I don't need to believe in souls to believe in soulmates."

Before I can offer a rebuttal to that very flawed argument, Dad presses the blender's "on" button, making so much noise I can barely hear myself think. I wince and clutch my throbbing temples.

For a second, he stops, but just as I open my mouth to say something, he starts the blender again.

"Very mature," I say when the blender is finally blessedly silent.

Feigning innocence, Dad pours the thick concoction into two mason jars, hands one to me, and covers the other with a lid.

Fighting my gag reflex, I take large sips of the "cure." It takes effort to keep it down.

Harry pokes me with his nose.

"You won't like it," I tell him.

Harry wags his tail.

"Fine." Since it is safe for dogs, I give him some of my drink, and he downs it like it's the most delicious thing he's ever tasted.

"I'll feed you again when we get home," I say, unable to help a grin that tugs at my lips.

"You also should eat something," Dad says. "That works as well as the hangover cure."

I nod. "I had cereal earlier. For lunch, I was planning on making some Japanese food for me and Brooklyn."

Hearing her name, Harry wags his tail.

The nice-smelling dudette? Where is she? I haven't sniffed her in a century.

Dad's eyebrows go up high on his forehead. "You're cooking for her already?"

"So?"

Dad hands me the sealed jar. "Cooking is your love language."

"And reading all that girly stuff about love languages is *your* love language," I say and then wince because I didn't mean to remind Dad of Mom so casually.

She was super into this stuff.

Thankfully, Dad doesn't seem fazed. "I don't think you fully understand the concept," he says with a huff.

"Neither do you. The five languages are words of affirmation, quality time, gifts, acts of service, and physical touch."

Honestly, I'm just busting his balls at this point. When Mom was in the hospital, I read that same book to please her.

Dad puffs up like a peacock. "Cooking is both a gift and an act of service. Reading what your partner likes is—"

"Quality time," I chime in.

Dad sighs. "If there's one thing you got from your mother, it's the ability to win any argument."

On that note, I grab Harry and the other jar and skedaddle.

———

"Honey, I'm home," I shout when I enter my house, groceries in tow.

No reply.

Hmm. Is she still sleeping?

Maybe. Or maybe she woke up, decided last night was a mistake, and ran far away from here.

Dammit. Why does that thought upset me so much?

Leaving the food on the kitchen table, I brace myself and go look for Brooklyn.

Chapter Seventeen

BROOKLYN

"*I'm going to my volunteering gig, should be back around noon,*" Evan's note says.

But it's already past noon.

Where did he—

"There you are," Evan says, startling me.

I turn and take him in. And just like that, something flutters in my chest. Are these heart palpitations—a lesser-known hangover symptom? Also, my underwear suddenly feels damp and my nipples overly sensitive. Is a teenager's libido another side effect of excessive alcohol consumption?

"How are you?" Evan asks softly, studying me.

I wince. "Do you have a guillotine?"

He shows me the jar he's holding. "Drink this. It helped me, tremendously."

Hmm. If this is anything like the sunburn poultice, I'd better give it a try.

Cautiously, I approach him and reach for the jar. He

again smells alluringly like wax and the salty ocean, with a touch of starfruit. My head was already spinning, but the proximity of his big, masculine frame makes it—along with the dampness in my panties and the nipple situation —much worse.

As I grab the jar, our fingers brush, and I get a flash-back of last night, those same fingers all over my—

"Don't sniff it," Evan warns. "Just gulp."

"I bet you say that to all the girls." Ignoring my body's unruly reactions, I unscrew the jar.

If you were to put stinky cheese into a compost pile, a year later the contents would taste and smell a lot like this jar. But hey, after I take a swig, my libido calms the fuck down.

"I know it's bad," Evan says. "But my headache is gone."

"This may be a case of the cure being worse than the disease." And yet I force myself to take another swig.

Harry waltzes in and looks at me longingly.

"You're a weirdo," Evan says to him before turning to me. "Any chance you can share some with him? He tried it earlier and clearly liked it."

I poke my finger into the horribleness and let Harry lick it off, which the dog does with greedy enthusiasm.

Huh. I guess if sniffing butts is one's idea of fun, one's bar for what's gross is a bit lower than mine.

"Now what?" I ask when the jar is almost empty, and I can't even imagine stomaching another sip.

"Harry gets the rest," Evan says with a grin. "Mean-while, how about you and I get some lunch?"

"Sure." I don't feel particularly hungry, but more food should help with the hangover.

Hopefully.

Also, sitting down for a meal might give us a chance to discuss last night. Like, what did it mean?

We head to the kitchen, and I watch in fascination as Evan preps food for the two of us once again. He looks extremely sexy as he does it.

When the meal is ready, I taste it without really tasting it, but compliment the chef nevertheless.

"So," I say, unsure how to bring up the topic of yesterday. "The treasure hunt was sure a hoot. Right?"

Grr. That was pathetic.

But hey, Evan smiles, so that's something. "It really was," he says. "And if you're not feeling too hungover, I'd like to continue. Maybe head over to Marianna?"

So that's how he's playing it? Avoiding the topic.

He looks at me worriedly. "Is it too soon?"

"I guess I could go," I say. "But no drinking."

Evan winces. "Not even if I had a gun to my head."

"Do you think you can drive smoothly?" I ask. "A bump on the road might just make my brain explode."

"I'll be like that song," he says. "A smooth operator."

A song about a man who is good at playing women? Is Evan giving me a hint about last night?

As we eat our meal, I don't dare ask, and he doesn't volunteer any answers. Instead, we simply learn more about each other—and the same is true on the drive to our next treasure map destination.

I learn who Evan's first kiss was, and he learns about

Brian, the horror show that was my first boyfriend. I tell him about my friends, and he tells me about his, as well as his dad.

The whole car ride, I keep thinking that if I wanted to come clean about Reagan, this would be the perfect chance, but I can't bring myself to do so.

"Why here?" Evan asks when we pull up to the parking lot near the entrance to the famous caverns.

"Because one of the clues was the year soda was invented," I explain.

Evan arches an eyebrow.

I sigh. "This place has something called the Soda Straw Room."

"Ah."

Evan gets us a private tour to make sure we can do the sleuthing once underground. Our tour guide, with his long, shaggy hair, looks exactly like a Puli... or Reagan for that matter.

Actually, no. Reagan doesn't look like a Puli at all. In fact, no one has bred a dog cute enough to compare with my son. If they ever do, they'll make billions.

I'm startled out of my reverie by the tour guide's booming tone. I glance at Evan. Once again, I feel like we're on a date—and a nice one at that. Between the cool underground air, the drip of water, and the majestic stalactites and stalagmites, I half expect to see Tolkien dwarves just around the corner—and I love every second of it.

The problem is, when we reach the Soda Straw

Room (named that on account of all the tubular stalactites), there are no clues anywhere—and we look, hard.

"Maybe you'll want to check out some of our other famous spots?" the Puli suggests when we give up and look disappointed.

It doesn't hurt to check, so we let him take us around as he explains what each place is called and why. The tour turns out to be awesome, of course, but again, no clues are to be found in either the Great Room, the Drapery Room, or anywhere else.

"Ready to give up?" Evan asks when the Puli takes us back to the gift shop. "Or should I book another tour?"

"No. This is Flagler College all over again. I'm starting to think you chose the wrong person to help you with the hunt."

Evan shakes his head. "You're doing much better than I did. Besides, we've got two more locations to check out."

"Fair." I step outside and wait for Evan to join me.

"How's your headache?" he asks after he exits. "I'm not sure if it was the cave air, Dad's cure, the food, or simply time, but mine is completely gone."

Huh. "Mine is gone too."

"Great." He gestures into the distance. "Did you know you can rent kayaks nearby?"

"You can?" And why is this topic making my heart flutter?

I glance at my tracker as if checking the time, but really it's to see if my heartrate is elevated—and it is.

My dear Precious, your heart is a nine-ounce marvel

in this universe of madness and darkness, and I squeal in
ecstasy with its every luscious pump.

"Yep," Evan says. "There are kayaks and boats. And
I'm not sure if I told you this, but I love kayaks... only no
one ever wants to ride them with me."

There it is. Until now, I could tell myself we were on
a treasure hunt, but if we go do *this* activity, that will be a
lot closer to a date—so I should say no. Right? But I
came here on vacation, and I've always wanted to try
kayaking, so I tell Evan that I'd be happy to join him.

"Yes!" Evan is so psyched that I start to wonder if he
really meant it when he said no one ever wants to go
with him.

In any case, he gets the kayak and sits in the front.

Oh, boy. Even with the life jacket over his T-shirt, I
can see his muscles work as he rows, which seriously
distracts me from the greenery and the calm waters. Still,
I feel myself de-stressing, all the tensions—except for the
sexual one—leaving my body with every stroke of the
paddles.

Soon, we spot an otter. And a manatee after that—
not to mention a number of turtles and different birds.

"I love kayaking," I say when we're done. "Who
knew?"

Evan beams at me. "I'm glad to hear that."

"My friends—the ones who booked me this vacation
—will be very happy to know I got to properly relax."
And they'll insist Evan deserves a reward for making it
happen. A lewd reward.

"But the day isn't over," Evan says. "Want to check out some local sights?"

He starts walking excitedly before I even voice my agreement, and I almost grab his hand as I fall into step beside him. Thankfully, I stop myself because—for the millionth time—this isn't an actual date.

Unless it is? No idea, but soon, I'm having too much fun to worry about the status of our relationship, and I only return to those thoughts on the drive back.

"How do you feel about eating out at some nice place on the way?" Evan asks and then lists a few options, all of which sound very fancy.

Eat somewhere nice? Again?

That's it.

I can't hold it in anymore.

"Are we on a date?"

Chapter Eighteen

EVAN

"**A**re we on a date?" Brooklyn demands.

What a great question—and how like a New Yorker to go straight for the jugular.

The truth is, this is something I've been ruminating on, like Calvin's cows do with the seaweed that washes onto the beach. Something about the seaweed makes them not fart, but I'm not sure I have anything to show for *my* ruminatory efforts because I'm as unprepared for Brooklyn's question now as I would have been this morning.

Well, except for one thing.

I've realized that I want her—despite all the reasons for us not to be together.

I want her badly. I want her in my bed. I want her in my life. I want to take her to more new places, so I can see that excited expression on her face. Not to mention—

"I'll take your silence as a no," Brooklyn says.

Grr. I take the first exit I see, pull into the parking lot

of the nicest-looking restaurant around, and then face her. "You're wrong."

She blinks at me. "I am?"

"I would like to go on a date with you."

As she bats her eyelashes at me, I can't help but notice how pretty they are. "I thought you didn't date tourists," she says.

Good point. "But I can always make an exception for someone who's *that* good at Scrabble."

Seriously, though, I'm having trouble remembering why I came up with that stupid rule. In a way, having a time limit on the relationship means that I don't have to tell Brooklyn about my vasectomy and therefore see the disappointment on her face. The time limit also means no one should get hurt. Especially if—

"So... it's a fling then?" she clarifies.

"Fling?" Yeesh. Why does the word bring the taste of the hangover cure to my mouth? "Do we have to put any labels on it? Let's just have dinner." I gesture at the rando place.

"Okay." She opens the car door. "Let's just have dinner."

After we sit down, the waiter dude walks over to us and sighs. "I'm not giving you any menus."

Hmm. Weird.

"Why not?" Brooklyn asks.

"We only have ingredients for a single item—a burger." He crosses his arms over his chest. "Before you ask, that doesn't mean cheeseburger, or a chickenburger, or a fish burger, or a veggie burger. Just a beef burger, with fries. That's it. No bacon. No—"

Brooklyn and I exchange confused glances.

"You want a burger?" I ask her, sounding uncertain.

"Do you?" she asks.

"Sure." I don't, but I don't want to start this dinner by being a dick to the waiter... even if it seems like he might deserve it.

"Two burgers," Brooklyn says. "You *do* have enough ingredients for two, right?"

Oh, yeah. He did make that burger sound pretty singular earlier. This attention to detail is why Brooklyn is so good at Scrabble.

"We can make two more burgers," the waiter says, but he doesn't sound all that sure. "They will have to be without any lettuce or tomato. Oh, and there's only one pickle left."

Damn it. Is it too late to—

"We're okay sharing that last pickle," Brooklyn says. When the waiter leaves, she whispers, "Doesn't it feel like we're in a pickle?"

I glance at a nearby table where the waiter is bringing an older lady her food—a burger, of course. As soon as he leaves, she pulls out a slice of American cheese from her purse and furtively sticks it under the bun.

"Wow," Brooklyn whispers, following my gaze. "They lack cheese and other accoutrements so often that the regulars bring their own."

I lean in. "Either that or this lady carries cheese everywhere she goes."

Brooklyn leans toward me as well. "I would've brought a tomato in her shoes."

Wow. We're so close I feel trapped by her gravitational field. Again. My eyes zero in on her lips, and I'm slowly drawn toward them. But before I reach my destination, Brooklyn pulls away with a chuckle.

"I just realized that I made it sound like I want us to use that lady as a mule," she says. "By forcing her to hide a tomato in her shoes."

I smile, partially to hide my kiss-deprivation disappointment. "I give it a few days before the waiter starts to check everyone's shoes for contraband."

Brooklyn snorts, but before I can make any more jokes at the waiter's expense, he's back with two plates.

Hey, one benefit of there not being any choices is that the one item they do have comes out pretty fast. And it smells good.

"Can I have a fork?" Brooklyn points at the French fries on her plate.

"We don't have forks," the waiter states.

"Hmm," Brooklyn says. "Do you have a spork or a spoon?"

"We don't have spoons," the waiter deadpans. "And no sporks."

Brooklyn sighs. "All right, I guess."

When the waiter leaves, she asks, "Are we still tipping that guy?"

"Hold that thought," I say. "There are better questions that have to be answered first."

She rolls her eyes. "Let me guess: Who eats fries with a fork?"

"Oh, that one will have to wait its turn," I say with a grin. "I'm much more curious as to what you would have done with a spoon."

Her shoulders bob. "I don't like grease on my fingers. Sue me."

"But a spoon—"

"Can work in a pinch," she says. "If you're willing to mush the fries, that is."

"Yuck. Fine. What about the burger?"

She straightens her spine. "What about it?"

"Do you hold the burger in your hands, or eat it with a fork, like a pervert? And how would you eat it with a spoon?"

With a small eyeroll, she grabs the burger and takes a big bite.

"Very mature," I say and follow her lead.

Wow. It's a good, juicy burger.

She must like it too because she arches an eyebrow at me before she grabs a handful of fries and stuffs them in after the burger, fingers dripping with grease. "Is this what you wanted?" she demands.

"Umm. Is it weird that it's actually hot?"

"Very," she says.

"Oh, well. It is." And I'm not lying one bit.

Grinning, she devours her food and excuses herself to go wash the grease off her hands.

I visit the men's room as well, figuring that since she has a thing against grease, I'd better rid myself of mine so as not to gross her out when I touch her. Wait, what am I saying? You don't want greasy hands in general.

When I get back to the table, Brooklyn is there, and so is the check.

I sigh. She's pitched in half the money.

"I know we're not putting labels on things," I say. "But we did say this was a date—and when I take someone out, I insist on paying."

Her expression turns mutinous. "And when is it going to be my turn to take you out?"

Grr. I wasn't going to do this, but given that we're on a date after having spent the night together, it's best to put this out in the open.

"I'd rather it never be your turn," I say. "But not because I'm trying to be one of those guys. It's more because I want to take you to pricey places that have more than burgers on the menu—places that would be trivial for me to afford, but that might strain *your* wallet."

She huffs. "How much do you make from that Airbnb?"

"It's not just that," I say. "Or the land I own. My grandpa also left me money—money that I invested in Octothorpe stock at a very opportune time."

Forehead furrowing, she displays her slender wrist to me. "I have an Octothorpe Glorp."

"Ah. Yeah. Octothorpe also makes lots of other technology," I say. Then, in case she hasn't heard, I add, "Their stock grew exponentially after the company went public. They are worth more than Apple, Google,

Amazon, and Microsoft combined. And they gave early investors their cryptocurrency as a—"

"You're super rich?" she asks, eyes wide.

I shrug. "What's considered *super* rich?"

Grudgingly, she picks up her cash. "A millionaire?"

"I'm not actually sure if I'm still a millionaire. Not after the recent market shift." I take my phone out to check my portfolio. "Yep. Apparently, I've just crossed into billionaire territory."

She drops the bills she picked up. "A billionaire?"

The cheese lady looks pointedly our way.

I shift in my seat uncomfortably. "Why not post it on social media while you're at it?"

"Sorry," Brooklyn says in a softer voice. "I'm just wrapping my brain around it. No offense, but you don't seem like a billionaire at all."

Right. She thought I was a plumber. Teasingly, I ask, "Do I have to buy the obligatory private jet for you to believe me?"

"Or a limo," she says. "Or a mansion."

I pick up her cash and hand it back to her. "I told you. I want a simple life. A farm by the ocean. That's about it."

"That's crazy," she says. "How can someone who's got all this money not want to spend it?"

"I do spend it," I say. "I donate to causes I believe in. Whenever my dad or I want something, I buy whatever it is without a second thought. I guess he and I just don't really need much to be happy, but I believe that goes for everyone else too. A person just needs some basic minimum income to pay all their bills and do their hobbies and things like that, but after that, more money doesn't do much." I take a deep breath before admitting in a quieter voice, "No amount of money was able to save my mom."

Shit. Why did I go there?

There's pity in Brooklyn's eyes, which wasn't my intention. But then she covers my hand with hers, and that feels nice. It brings me out of the temporary funk I got into.

"So." I clear my throat. "Will you finally let me pay for the dates I take you on?"

She nods. "But on one condition: you have to let me groom your pets as a thank-you."

I wince. "Sure, but only Harry. Sally would slice your veins open if you tried."

She sits up. "You let me worry about Sally."

"Those"—I drop a wad of cash on the table—"are famous last words."

———

"I'm curious about something," Brooklyn says as we start driving. "But it's not a polite question."

I glance at her. "Is it polite to tease someone the way you're doing right now?"

"Fine. You're attractive."

"Thanks," I say with a grin.

"And obscenely rich," she adds.

"And?" I think I know where this is going.

"How come you're single?" she demands, confirming my suspicion. "When I think 'billionaire,' I think 'arm candy.'"

I grin. "Like you."

"I'm serious," she says, but she doesn't look very serious.

"My being rich isn't really a variable when it comes to my dating life," I say. "I don't share that fact with a lot of people in general, but especially not with women."

Except this one.

Once again, she looks at me like I've grown a dick outside of the usual location. "Why not?"

"I'm not interested in women who'd want a man for his money," I say.

"Oh." She scratches her head. "I guess that makes sense."

Should I tell her about my inability to give someone a child? I doubt a better chance will present itself. "Why are *you* single?" I ask instead. "You're smart, funny, attractive, and—"

"Don't try to change the subject," she says.

"Right back at you."

"Forget it. I've just figured out why you're single. You're an ass."

"Huh. I think it's the opposite for you."

Her eyebrow asks the obvious question.

"Your nice ass is why I can't believe you're single."

She chuckles but steers the conversation away, which is just fine with me. Instead, by the time we reach my community, I've learned that she describes people in terms of dog breeds they resemble, and I've told her how easily I can get hangry—case in point, our initial meeting.

"Yeah, I get like that when I have my period," she blurts as we pull up to my driveway. "Which was the case that day."

Oh. "That explains things."

Her eyes go squinty. "What's that supposed to mean?"

I put the car in park, jump out, and open the door for her. "I'm just kidding."

She takes my proffered hand. "I am too."

As we touch, a montage of the events from last night plays in front of my eyes (or is it my dick?), and I'm instantly hard.

"So." Brooklyn glances at the rental and then at my place. "What happens after a date without labels?"

"This." I claim her lips with a kiss.

Chapter Nineteen

BROOKLYN

Oh, my. I thought the vodka was why kissing Evan last night felt out of this world. How else could it have been so good? But today, I'm stone-cold sober, and this is still the best kiss of my life. A ruining kiss too, which sucks because labels or not, whatever this is we're not labeling is going to be short.

After what feels like an hour of bliss, I pull away and look up at Evan expectantly. On the one hand, I want to be invited in, but on the other, I—

"You still want to groom Harry?" Evan absentmindedly touches his lips.

Huh. I pull myself together since it sounds like I'm needed in a professional capacity. "I want to groom Harry *and* Sally."

He shakes his head. "Just the dog. You don't need another trip to the hospital."

"How about I do Sally tomorrow and Harry today?"

I suggest. Yeah. Great thinking. That leaves me more time to do Evan tonight if it comes to that.

"Deal." Evan grabs my hand and leads me toward his front door, which makes me feel very melty in the region of my panties—something I've never felt before a pet grooming.

When the door opens, Harry greets us excitedly.

"Hey, bud." Evan releases my hand and ruffles Harry's fur. "You're about to get a treat."

Ah. The grooming, right. That was the pretext for coming over. "How do you usually wash Harry?" I ask Evan.

Evan grins. "Hose, outside. Or one of those showers at the beach. But he considers baths a treat, so I think that might be the way to go in this case."

Aha. Bath. "Want to help me?"

Evan nods. "Come on, bud, let's take a bath."

Harry is so happy you'd think Evan told him he's just inherited a peanut butter factory.

As soon as we get Harry into the bath and turn on the shower, the dog looks blissed out—but then he performs a shake out his kind is so good at.

Evan laughs. "This is why I don't do this often."

Yeah. Evan and I are now wet, with me in multiple senses of the word courtesy of Evan's bulging muscles peeking through his wet shirt. My own shirt is soaked and therefore sheer, which Evan clearly notices and is happy to see. That, or he must bring a rather large flashlight to all of his pet-grooming sessions.

Gritting my teeth, I do my best to stay professional as I proceed with the wash.

Nope. This is not even close to professional. Evan is so adorable with his fur baby that it makes me think of the one thing Reagan has never gotten to experience—having a dad. And picturing Evan in the role of a dad is a bad, bad idea.

Note to self: Avoid doing such domestic crap with flings or guys with whom one is doing stuff with no labels. Granted, this is a pretty useless note because I'm not normally interested in flings or label-less whatevers.

When the bathing is done but before we can properly towel him off, Harry runs around the house like he's on fire instead of wet, and Sally watches his antics with a sinister expression that seems to say, "Go ahead. Try getting me wet. See what happens."

Hmm. Could Sally be impervious to my cat tricks? Whatever. For now, I need to finish dealing with Harry, so with Evan's help, I catch him and start to detangle his fur.

"Wow," Evan says when I manage to rid Harry of a piece of gum that was stuck in his fur for what looks like a year. "You're the best groomer I've ever met."

Hey, maybe causing myself to smell like a wet dog was worth it. "Harry seems to be free of any parasites. Want to help me trim his nails?"

Evan agrees, so we do Harry's mani-pedi and then jointly brush his teeth.

"Your breath smells amazing," Evan says afterward.

"Thanks," I say.

"I was talking to Harry," Evan says with a grin. "But yours smells even better."

Before I can reply, Harry decides that the compliment is a great excuse to give Evan a doggy kiss.

Hey. Unfair. I had the same idea. Though maybe with less tongue.

Done going to first base with his dog, Evan looks at me sheepishly. "I'll go brush my teeth... just in case."

"I don't find dog kisses gross." To prove my point, I let Harry place one on me.

"Well," Evan says. "I kind of do, so..."

"This from the guy who gave me crap about greasy hands?"

Evan rolls his eyes. "I'm brushing my teeth. You don't have to."

"No, I will," I say magnanimously.

"Thank you." Evan waves for me to follow and leads me into his bedroom.

When I spot his bed, my heart skips a few beats.

We walk into the bathroom together and brush our teeth—another little bit of domesticity that makes something ache in my chest.

Damn. How can someone brush his teeth so sexily? Given the purpose of the activity, you'd think it would be utilitarian at most.

With effort, I focus on taking care of the doggie cooties in my mouth, but I can't help catching Evan's gaze in the mirror a few times. A gaze that's hard to decipher.

"Can I use your shower?" I gesture at my wet clothes. "And maybe get something to wear?"

This time, Evan's expression is a lot clearer. "Sure..." His voice is husky. "Do you need help soaping your back?"

Before I can give this due consideration, my head is already bobbing in the affirmative.

Smiling crookedly, Evan begins to strip in the same showy fashion that he did yesterday after losing at Scrabble.

Mouth open, I watch the show all the way to the end, where Vitamin D makes its very big comeback.

"Your turn." Evan turns away and approaches the shower.

Oh, my. Evan's powerful back and muscular butt are mouthwatering. And pussywatering.

Evan turns on the shower.

I realize I haven't blinked this whole time, so I allow myself a cat-like slow blink.

Evan turns back to me and frowns. "Look, Brooklyn, if you don't want to—"

I rip my shirt off my body with such haste you'd think it were acid and not water it's soaked in.

As I strip off the rest, Evan's eyes grow ever more hooded. After I slide my panties down, he closes the distance between us and gives me another mind-shattering kiss. Then, without releasing my lips, he carries me into the shower.

When the hot water hits my skin, hormones make things a little hazy for the next few seconds. There are definitely lots of soapy hands all over my body: one on my left breast, the second on my lower back, the third between my—

Wait. Third?

Ah, right. That's me, pressing firmly on my clit.

"That's right," Evan croons. "Make yourself come for me."

I'm not sure if it's his words or the pent-up sexual energy brought on by being around him for so long, but a powerful orgasm explodes in my core, making my legs wobble. Thankfully, Evan is there to hold me up.

"Good job." He puts my hand on the tile wall to the right of me. "Make sure you don't fall."

Yeah. Great idea. Wait, where is he—

"I want to taste you." He drags his tongue down my body as he gets on his knees.

Oh, fuck.

He cups my butt as his tongue flits over my still-over-sensitive clit.

I grip that tile wall for all its worth and grab Evan's hair with my other hand to keep myself stable.

"Just like that," he croons into my pussy, and the vibrations bring me to the brink of another orgasm.

I'm almost there when Evan slows down. Then he speeds up.

"No," I gasp. "Don't tease!" I pull him where I want him, and boy, does he get the message. Flattening his tongue, he presses it against my sex and pulls me toward him, fingers digging into my butt cheeks.

"Fuck," I moan as I convulse into his mouth.

He gets back on his feet. "Now I really ought to soap your back."

Oh? As Evan gets behind me, Vitamin D pokes me very intriguingly in the left butt cheek. Then Evan starts to lather my back, making it official: anywhere he touches becomes an erogenous zone.

When my back is done, Evan turns his attention to my butt—which feels amazing... at least until a soapy finger gently circles in the very middle.

"Do you like that?" he whispers into my ear.

"What?" I gasp.

He slides the tip of his finger into my back opening. "This?"

"I don't know." I'm intrigued but scared at the same time. "But I've never done anal if that's what you're asking."

Until this vacation, I didn't think I'd ever even consider it, but something about Evan brings out the adventuress in me. Case in point: until yesterday, I didn't think I'd ever play Strip Scrabble. Not that these two things are in the same league. Anal is—

"Let me try something," Evan murmurs and licks my neck.

Okay. That's nice. That I definitely like. More than like.

He gently positions me facing the wall, legs spread, both hands on the tile wall—like he might fuck me from behind.

My heartbeat skyrockets.

Is he going to just stick Vitamin D in my ass?

Wouldn't I need copious amounts of lube before attempting—

Nope. Evan nibbles his way down to my shoulder blades.

Wait. Is he—

Yep. Sliding his hands down the sides of my body, Evan licks down my spine, his tongue passing my coccyx bone and gliding down the crease between my butt cheeks until his tongue ends up where his finger was a moment ago as he grips the sides of my hips.

My entire body turns red hot and tingly with equal parts embarrassment and arousal. The actual sensation is tickly but nice. It's the knowledge of what he's doing that makes my heart pound and my cheeks burn. And I mean both sets of cheeks.

He makes a wide circle with his tongue. Then a smaller circle.

A giggle bubbles up in my throat.

Releasing my right hip, Evan caresses my clit with the tip of his finger.

The giggle fizzles out, replaced with a growing tension.

Upon completion of his smallest circle thus far, Evan slides the tip of his tongue into my back opening—just as the finger that was on my clit enters my pussy.

I gasp as my body tenses and all the earlier sensations intensify, with pleasure winning over embarrassment by a wide margin.

His tongue and finger penetrate me deeper, in and out, in a faster and faster rhythm.

A moan escapes my lips.

The rhythm intensifies.

"Yes!" I grip the tiles for all I'm worth.

Encouraged by my outcry, Evan starts fucking my ass with his tongue in earnest, just as his finger mercilessly locates what must be my g-spot—because an intense burst of pleasure explodes inside me, making me come as I scream his name.

"You're amazing," Evan croons. "Now turn toward me and lean against the wall."

I'm too overwhelmed to ask silly questions like "Why?" or "What are you going to do to me now?" Instead, I face him and watch, mesmerized, as he fists Vitamin D until he comes all over my belly.

And just like that, I'm ready to go again. It has something to do with the warmth of his seed on my skin, the expression on his face, and—

Evan grabs the shower gel and washes my stomach clean, then my breasts, paying close attention to my nipples.

I'm not just ready to go—I crave another orgasm like a junky her next fix.

"Here." Turning off the shower, Evan brings a finger to my mouth. "I'll need some lube for the next thing I want to try."

What thing? My mouth is a little dry as I suck the proffered finger, but my pussy is anything but.

Evan gets on his knees again and repeats his cunnilingual masterpiece, but with one crucial difference: the tip of the finger I just sucked enters my butt.

A moan is on my lips again, and my eyes roll into the back of my head. His finger feels very different from his tongue, but also nice, in a hot, dirty way. It's harder and seemingly thicker—a hint of how Vitamin D would feel.

Speaking of Evan's tongue, it's clever enough to file an orgasm-related patent with the USPTO. It makes me feel so good I back my butt into Evan's finger, taking it up to the second knuckle and loving every millimeter of it.

"Come." Evan's command propels my cresting orgasm over the edge, and I do as he says, clenching around Evan's finger like a Chinese trap.

Sliding his finger out, Evan kisses my neck, then whispers into my ear, "How was that?"

"Incredible." An understatement of the century. The truth is, if we had enough time to do what we're doing today for a few months, I think I could work up to anal —but alas, we have a few measly days left, and I plan on having Vitamin D exclusively in my pussy as often as I can.

Evan's smile is pure male satisfaction. "Want me to wash your hair?"

"Sure." I'm hoping that getting pampered will reverse the weird post-climax malaise that has just come over me, and it does, to a degree. A much better savior for my mood is the sleepiness that turns my body into wet papier-mâché.

"Take me to bed," I beg Evan when the suds are gone from my body. To punctuate my request, I yawn. Loudly.

Nodding, Evan gets me out of the shower, towels me off, and wraps himself around me on the bed—which is when I pass out.

————

When I wake up, Evan is not in the bed with me, and his side is cold.

Well, I'm not spiraling this time. Instead, I reach for the note on the nightstand.

Went to get breakfast. Will be back at 11.

Eleven? I check my phone. It's ten. I know it's silly, but I feel proud that I've managed to wake up while it's still considered morning. And I'm way more refreshed than when I slept to almost noon yesterday. I guess imbibing less gives you more restful sleep, as do multiple orgasms.

At the thought of said orgasms, I blush and get up.

After I make myself presentable, I prance over to the kitchen in order to greet Evan as soon as he returns. And that's where I witness an interesting scene: The cat meows pointedly at the sliding door. Harry waltzes over and paws at the locking mechanism, unlocking it. He then slides the door open with his nose just a small smidge, but it's all Sally needs to squeeze her head through, which she does. As soon as she's on the screened porch, Harry closes the door behind her, like nothing has happened.

"Is this how Sally gets into my rental?" I ask Harry sternly.

Harry wags his tail, eyes gleaming with seemingly genuine innocence.

"But that can't be," I say. "Unless you go with her to open the doors at my place?"

Harry cocks his head.

"Never mind." I reopen the door to the porch and try herding Sally back into the house.

Yeah, no. There's a good reason we compare impossible tasks to the herding of cats. It's a nightmare.

Returning to the kitchen, I rummage through all the drawers until I hit paydirt: dry catnip in a bag.

My grin is evil as I ready the stuff. If Sally is one of the many cats who respond to nepetalactone—which is a great Scrabble word and happens to be the chemical in catnip that gives felines a high—I will not only get her back into the house, but I will probably be able to groom her without risking life and limb. Hell, I could probably get her to use the bane of every cat's existence: a cat carrier.

Armed with the bait, I walk out onto the porch. "Hey, kitty. Your friendly neighborhood drug dealer is here."

Yep. Sally is clearly a junky already, which makes sense. Why else would Evan have it? Then again, if he has this, why can't he use it to give Sally a bath?

Soon, I find out why. Though Sally wants catnip enough to return to the house, she doesn't want it badly enough to get anywhere near the bathtub. All I manage to do with the catnip is brush and trim her fur in a few places—which, hey, is still grooming.

"I guess it's a good thing you don't actually need baths," I say to Sally when she hisses at my final attempt to give her a wash. "Not unless you fall into cold soup, like one of my client's cats did."

"You're lucky her claws didn't come out," Evan says from behind me. "I told you she doesn't like baths."

I spin around. "I didn't hear you come back."

"Sorry about that." He puts a shopping bag on the table. "In my defense, I wasn't being stealthy—you were just so preoccupied with grooming Sally that an elephant could've tumbled in."

"A sexy elephant." Wait, what?

Evan's forehead wrinkles. "Thanks?"

"What's for breakfast?" I demand grumpily.

Evan tells me, then prepares a Japanese-style omelet as I watch and drool.

When we start eating, I stare at his mouth, wondering if it was always this fascinating. I also blush every time I get a glimpse of his tongue because it reminds me of the dirty things he did with it last night. Things that—

"What are your thoughts?" Evan pours me some tea.

"I'm not going to be ready for anal," I blurt. "Not anytime soon."

"Good to know." Evan grins. "But I was asking as to your thoughts on whether we should drive to St. Petersburg or Miami today."

Even when he played with my butt last night, I don't think my cheeks turned *this* shade of crimson.

"Either one is fine," I mumble, wanting to sink through the floor. "Your choice."

"Then how about we head to St. Petersburg?" Evan says. "We can swing by the Salvador Dali Museum there. My grandfather was a big fan of his, so who knows, maybe that will somehow help you get a clue."

Get a clue is what I need to do before I talk about readiness for anal again. "What else was your grandfather into?"

Evan stands up. "Can I tell you on the way?"

"Sure. Do you have any photo albums, or anything else involving your grandfather?"

He smirks. "If you want to see baby pictures of me, just say so."

Rolling my eyes, I help him fill the dishwasher—another domestic task that leaves me feeling unsettled. Afterward, I swing by my place to change, and when I join him in the car, he hands me a photo album.

Score! There are uber-cute baby pictures of Evan. In some, he is with his mom, and in others with his dad—whom he resembles quite a bit. I know how much his mom means to him, so I ask questions about the memories captured in these photos, and he tells me all about the many special moments he shared with her growing up. The grandfather pics are a minority here, but I do locate some, including one at some formal event where he is hugging Evan.

Damn. My mouth waters as I take in Evan in a tux, tie, and what looks like an obscenely expensive watch on his wrist.

Looking at this image, it's easy to believe that Evan is a billionaire, which is funny since at the time of this event, I don't believe he was.

Is it shallow that this picture makes me like Evan even more? Does it mean I like Evan being a billionaire? That would make me one of the gold-digging types he's been avoiding—yet another reason for us not to be together, not that we need more.

Actually, I've got to give myself a break. I don't *really* care about his money. I just find him hot in a suit, not to mention my perception of him is now colored by what happened in the shower. And during all the dates. And the—

"Did the pictures reveal any clues?" Evan asks.

"Not really," I say, snapping back to reality.

"Oh, well," he says. "It was worth a shot."

I close the album. "Can you tell me something about your grandfather?"

He concentrates. "I got my love of the ocean from him."

"Did he surf too?"

Evan shakes his head. "He just liked to watch the waves. It calmed him."

For the rest of the ride, he tells me about his grandfather, but nothing really gives me any clues. What I get instead is an aching in my chest. I've been estranged from my family for seven years, but even prior to that, I never had as good of a connection with them as Evan had with his grandfather. And his father. And his mother.

"We're here." Evan turns into a parking lot, and we

take a stroll through the gorgeous gardens—one of the oldest roadside tourist attractions in the US.

As we scour the grounds, my enjoyment of the day fights with frustration because once again, there are no clues. Additionally, a double dose of guilt tugs at my insides. Firstly, Reagan would really enjoy this place. Secondly, I still haven't told Evan about Reagan's existence.

"Maybe we'll find some in Miami?" Evan suggests when I voice my annoyance at the lack of clues.

"Maybe."

He gestures at the nature around us. "Wasn't this place worth visiting, even if there are no clues?"

I take in the greens of the plants and the pinks of the flamingoes nearby. "It's a nice place, but—"

"No buts." Evan grabs my hand. "Let's go through it again, forgetting about clues altogether."

At first, I walk to indulge him, but soon, I do forget about the treasure hunt and start to feel like I'm on one of the best dates of my life.

"Want to take a seat?" Evan gestures at a bench that seems lost in the greenery.

Take a seat? I guess we did walk a while. I glance at my tracker to see how many steps I already took, and it's a whopping ten thousand.

My dear Precious, your majestic glutes are getting firmer as we speak, and your thighs are becoming adamantine. You're also producing rich sweat and delectable lactic acid all over the sacred shrine that is your body.

I guess I could relax my feet for a second.

I plop on the bench, and Evan cozies up right next to me.

Wait. Is he—

He wraps his hand around my shoulders, his nearness intoxicating.

"We seem to be alone," he murmurs, his lips brushing my ear enticingly.

I scan the paved path in both directions. It's true that at the moment, we're alone. But why do I have a feeling that he has something very naughty in mind that—

His lips clash with mine.

There it is.

Saw it coming, but that doesn't make it any less hot —or welcome.

As his tongue explores my mouth, I experience déjà vu. I either had a wet dream that started just like this, or saw a couple kissing on a garden bench in a movie. But then Evan's hand slides between my legs, pressing on my clit through my yoga pants. That's not from a movie, that's for sure. Not unless it was porn.

I give my brain a command to say something about us being in public, but a soft moan escapes my mouth instead.

"Yes." Evan kisses my neck. "Lean into the feeling."

Lean in? More like I'm about to drop off a cliff. A tension starts to coil in my core and—

A male park employee who resembles a Neapolitan Mastiff appears on the path nearby, frowning at us.

All the blood from my clit rushes into my face as I leap to my feet.

"Why don't you get a room?" the employee says gruffly with such annoyance that it makes me wonder if his job happens to be chasing would-be lovers from this exact bench.

Evan stands up to his full height, towering over the newcomer. "Why don't you watch your tone?"

Is this like that time he was upset with Dr. Hugo? Something to do with the Y chromosome?

"I think you should leave." The park dude reaches for his walkie-talkie as if it were a gun.

Before Evan does something even more male and therefore stupid, I grab his hand. "I want to see the Dali Museum anyway," I whisper in his ear. "Let's get the hell out of here."

Calming instantly, Evan nods, and we head out.

"Here." I grab Evan a Snickers at the gift shop. "I think you're in a hangry mood."

"You might have a point." Evan stuffs the whole bar into his mouth and chews as we get into our car. "Sorry about that," he says once we're on the road.

"Don't apologize." I grin. "I find it flattering that you can't keep your hands off me."

"Yeah." The corners of his lips lift. "I'm just *that* turned on by how modest you are."

"Do you want to grab some more food to make sure you don't kill someone at the museum?"

He shakes his head. "We're almost there, and they have a very nice café."

Turns out, nice is an understatement. Café Gala, named after the Russian woman who was Dali's wife and muse, features Spanish food and an amazing ambience.

"These are actual tapas," Evan says when we get some. "Notice how little they resemble a Japanese breakfast?"

"Well, then, eat your tapas and fast." I dump spiced almonds and mixed olives onto his plate. "Hanger is still making you too prickly for my liking."

"I'll get you for this," Evan says and stuffs his mouth.

———

After our bellies are full, we walk around, looking at surrealistic art—an activity I really enjoy, though more due to Evan's company than any real appreciation of the nuances of Dali's work.

Then a small piece catches my attention for some reason. In it, a woman's body seems to be melting next to a violin, a horse is jumping out of a barrel, and an angel is looking at all this and rubbing his eyes.

"Ah, this one," Evan says. "You should see it upside down."

I drag my gaze away from the painting. "What?"

"This piece is famous for looking completely different when turned upside down. Half the time, they hang it that way, and half the time this way—the inferior way."

Really? I tilt my head, but the sideways view doesn't show me what Evan is talking about.

"Do you need help?" Evan asks.

"With what?"

He pantomimes turning a beach ball in his hands—that or milking a giant cow. "Help getting upside down. So you can see it."

I blink. "You can do that?"

He flexes his bicep. "What, you don't think I'm strong enough?"

"It's not that..."

He walks up to me. "Enjoy." He grabs me around my knees with one arm and around my midsection with the other, and then, without any effort, he's got me upside down, dangling like an idiot.

"What do you think?" He lifts me up a little and points me at the painting. "Can you see the secret image?"

Hmm. The melty face looks more like a face, and there's a spider on her cheek, but I could've seen that standing upright. I just didn't get the chance.

"What are you doing?" someone demands.

Evan turns, allowing me to see one of the security people—a lady who strongly resembles a Brussels Griffon.

"I'm just looking at the painting upside down," I explain matter-of-factly.

The Brussels Griffon frowns. "Why?"

"This is a special painting," I explain.

"No. It's not."

Evan chuckles.

Glaring up at him, I demand that he put me down, which he does and starts cracking up in earnest.

"Please behave with some decorum from now on," the Griffon says sternly.

"Sorry," Evan says. "She will."

The Griffon leaves.

I glare at Evan. "Not cool."

"I told you I'd get you," he says with a smirk. "And I did."

"Whatever."

He chuckles again. "You realize you could've taken a picture of the painting and turned *that* upside down."

I punch him in the shoulder and walk over to check out more paintings. Soon, we run out of art to gawk at, so we go outside and get lost in a hedge maze—and kiss when we find the center, though Evan keeps it PG this time on account of the voices of children nearby.

"Where to now?" I ask when we exit the maze.

He shrugs. "Want to check out downtown?"

I do, so we head there before touring a gallery, followed by dinner and a walk on the beach.

"The sunsets are gorgeous here," Evan says. "The sun sets into the ocean."

"Yes, yes," I say mockingly. "This is the most romantic date of my life as is. Now you're just overselling it."

Wait, can I call it a date with the whole 'no labels' business still in play?

Evan smiles at me, but then he frowns at something at his feet.

What the hell? He seems to be upset over an empty plastic water bottle. Muttering a curse, he picks up the bottle and a plastic shovel that a kid must've left behind after making sandcastles.

"This sunset will really up the bar in the romance department," he says, resuming our walk while holding the garbage like nothing is amiss. "I guarantee it."

"You missed something." I point at an ice cream wrapper a few feet away.

"Ah." Evan picks up the wrapper. "Thank you."

"A billionaire who doubles as a beach cleaner?"

He shrugs. "I'd rather be that than a beach bum... a moniker I've gotten in the past."

Spotting something in the distance, he strides there intently, and I follow.

The something turns out to be a trash can. Evan deposits his haul into it, then picks up a candy wrapper that missed the trash and drops it where it should've gone.

When he resumes our walk on the beach like nothing's the matter, I blurt, "Do you have OCD?"

His house *was* pretty clean. As was my rental.

He shakes his head. "I just don't like to see the ocean polluted, that's all."

Ah. Makes sense now that he mentions it. "Given your money and all, wouldn't it make more sense for you to hire people to clean the beaches instead of doing it yourself?"

"I kind of do," he says. "Not directly, but some of the causes I donate to do that."

Now that he's reminded me, I'm curious about the causes he supports, so I quiz him about it for a while.

There is a definite pattern to his philanthropy, and even when the cause isn't directly related to the ocean, it's still tangentially related. For example, he donates to research projects that work on biodegradable materials.

"Want to have a seat there?" Evan points at a pristine patch of white-as-snow sand.

"Did you call ahead and get someone to clean up this spot?" I plop down and luxuriate in the feeling of warm sand on my toes.

As Evan joins me, he sits so close that our elbows brush each other—which wakes horny butterflies in my belly... and lower too. Despite all the sun exposure I've had today, I'm still in desperate need of some Vitamin D.

"That's the Palace." He gestures at a castle-like struc-ture behind us. At my confused expression, he says, "It's part of the most expensive hotel chain in the world, so its portion of the beach is kept pristine."

Before I can reply, the sky catches my attention and renders me momentarily speechless. The setting sun has painted the clouds with a glorious mixture of purple and orange that belongs more in a surrealistic Dali painting than in the real world.

"You weren't kidding about the sunsets," I gasp.

He puts his arm around my shoulders. "It would've been worth the drive just to see this, right?"

"Yeah." But I'd take that logic a few steps further. It was worth going on vacation—with a flight from New York and everything—just to experience this moment of pure contentment in Evan's embrace.

But that special moment is fleeting because I

remember that my vacation is ending very soon. And my time with Evan. And—

"So beautiful," Evan murmurs.

I turn his way and realize he's looking at me, not at the sunset.

I moisten my suddenly dry lips. "If you hadn't gotten there already, I'd suspect you're trying to get into my pants."

A charming smirk is his reply. Then he closes the small distance between us and claims my lips in a searing, heart-stealing kiss.

Chapter Twenty

EVAN

Brooklyn's lips might be my favorite thing about her, right after her quirky sense of humor, her love of animals, her perfect tits, her amazing ass, her pink—

She pulls away from my kiss, and I see why: an elderly couple are walking our way down the shore, holding hands.

Fucking adorable cockblockers. Flaunting a long and happily married life and therefore highlighting the transience of our 'no labels' whatever-it-is.

Damn it. I've been yo-yoing from happy to heavy-hearted all day long, and all for the stupidest reason: I'm really, really enjoying my time with Brooklyn... who is leaving soon.

Why can't this be like riding a great wave? When I do that, I live in the moment, enjoying being with one the ocean and the world. What I don't do is mourn the fact that the wave is about to disappear—because all waves do.

Brooklyn clears her throat. "Shouldn't we head back? The ride here was pretty long."

Great point. "Do you want to stay here for the night?"

Shit. That was definitely my dick talking.

"Where?" Brooklyn looks around as if I were suggesting we sleep here on the beach.

And hey, if it weren't for elderly cockblocking couples and sand sneaking into the most private of places, that option would be pretty romantic.

"The Palace?" I point in its direction. As I try to sell her on the idea, I like it more and more. "It's actually a really cool place, so this way, we'll cram yet another experience into this already-awesome day." Is my cock making me sound like a travel agent? "Also, if we stay here, we can head out in the morning and be in Miami by lunch." Yeah. It's more efficient for the treasure hunt. My offer has nothing to do with the fact that I (and more importantly, my dick) can't wait for the long ride back to be alone with her.

"Sure." Brooklyn stands up. "Let's go."

I leap to my feet as though an angler fish has just jumped out of the ocean and threatened my blue balls. And I can't believe my luck. When I suggested we go to the hotel, I meant after the obligatory wait for the gorgeous sunset to be over. But I'm not going to look this gift horse in the pussy.

I mean mouth.

Fucker.

Did that proverb always have undertones of bestiality?

Brooklyn grabs my hand, snapping me back to reality. Her palm is tiny in mine, and so soft and warm, making it all too easy to imagine it on my—

"Have you stayed at the Palace before?" she asks.

I nod. "The one in New York. I was there for an investor conference organized by Octothorpe."

She looks thoughtful at this. Is she picturing what it would have been like if I'd met her while I was at that conference? She lives in Brooklyn, so it was theoretically possible for us to have met. I went out to get pizza at—

"Have you been to New York since?" she asks.

"Twice. At that same conference, I met Mason—a video call drinking buddy who, if he lived in Florida, would probably become my best friend."

She grins. "I have two very close friends, and I think they each think they are my best friend, but I care for them equally."

"To slightly paraphrase the Highlander: there can be only one best friend."

Her grin turns impish. "Maybe I should give Jolene and Dorothy swords and have them duel for the honor."

The rest of the way to the hotel, she tells me about her friends and how they got her this trip as a birthday present.

"I changed my mind," I tell her when we reach the hotel door. "Both of them deserve the 'best' moniker."

"Agreed," she says, and we enter the hotel lobby,

which turns out to be a carbon copy of the one in New York: same exotic birds, same mixture of different European architectural styles, and same porters dressed in capes, bicorns, and garish pantaloons.

"You were right," Brooklyn whispers. "This *was* worth visiting."

I gently squeeze her hand, which I'm still holding.

A snooty concierge glares at the sand we're trekking into the lobby—like he hasn't seen people return from the beach a million times by now.

"Hello," I say to him. "We'd like a room."

The guy looks me over and doesn't seem impressed. "We're not running any discounts at the moment."

A kindling of annoyance sneaks through my Brooklyn-induced hormone overdose. It feels a lot like when I'm about to get hangry, which makes sense, because I am starving for something—it just doesn't happen to be food. "I don't need any discounts," I say coolly. "Just give me the first available room."

Looking doubtful, the concierge lazily types something into his computer, then looks back up with the fakest apologetic expression I've ever seen in my life. "I'm afraid all our *regular* rooms are booked."

Is my eye twitching? "Why did you emphasize 'regular?' Are 'special' rooms available?"

"Well, rooms like the penthouse are—"

"I'll take it." I get my wallet and rummage for my credit card.

The concierge rolls his eyes. "The penthouse costs—"

His words are cut off when he spots my American Express Black Card.

"Oh." His whole demeaner changes in an eyeblink. "Do you want the suite with the pool?"

"Yes."

"What about—"

"Stop wasting time," I grit out. "I'll take the best damned suite available. Now." I toss the card at the guy as if it were a ninja star.

"Okay." He catches the card with such adroitness it makes me wonder how often other people have tossed cards at him. "I'll book you into the Royal Suite."

Brooklyn arches an eyebrow at me, so I wink back, my annoyance fading.

When we get into the elevator, she blurts, "Something is wrong with me."

"Why?"

She blushes. "When you grumped at that dumbass, I found it kind of hot."

"Pervert," I say with a smile. "Seriously, though, I'm sorry about that. I'm not usually so easy to rile up."

"Are you sure?" She grins. "What if you're low on calories?"

"Well, I'm not craving food right now." I lean in and whisper into her ear, "But I am ravenous."

Her cheeks turn their deepest pink yet, which was my intent. "I think I'm hungry for that too."

Fuck me. My erection is borderline painful now.

Beast mode activating, I gather Brooklyn into my

arms and kiss her roughly and deeply, doing with my tongue what I'm dying to do with my cock.

Brooklyn melts into me, her soft parts feeling glorious on all my hard ones.

The elevator seems to slow to a crawl—it's clearly a cockblocker, like those old people on the beach.

When I'm on the verge of bursting, the doors finally open into the luxurious suite, which could be a hovel for all I care, so long as there is a bed. Or a carpet. Or a wall. Honestly, even a cement floor would work as long as no old people barge in on us.

In our frantic quest to get naked, we sprinkle clothes onto the floor as we search for the abovementioned bed, and when we locate our quarry, Brooklyn pulls away from my kiss to whistle appreciatively. "This bed is enormous." She glances down at my hard cock and grins wickedly. "Sorry, I should probably reserve that adjective for *that*. The bed is merely huge."

I pull her so close my cock touches the luscious skin just below her navel. "Are you trying to stroke my ego?"

Her wicked grin becomes devilish as Brooklyn reaches down and strokes my dick, once, twice. "Do or do not," she says in a Yoda impersonation. "There is no try."

My cock twitches in her hand, and if I were to suddenly develop a fetish for Yoda cosplay after this, I wouldn't be surprised.

"Oh, I don't plan to try," I murmur, staring down at her. "I'll *do* you so hard you'll be screaming my name."

Her reply is to stroke me again, squeezing lightly as she does.

My balls tighten—and no doubt turn a bluer hue. "Get on the bed," I order gruffly. "And spread your legs for me."

Fucking fuck. I owe our "merely" huge bed a debt of gratitude because in order to do as I say, Brooklyn has to crawl on all fours for a few feet—and it's the most erotic thing I've ever seen.

With hands unsteady from all the pent-up sexual energy, I ready a condom and leap after Brooklyn, or more specifically, after her delectable pink pussy.

Greedily, I flip her so she's face up, then lick her clit and suck on her folds until she comes all over my mouth with a loud moan that reverberates through my cock and balls.

All right. If I don't fuck her soon, I might actually turn sex-crazed. And yet, as if to torture myself, I penetrate her with a finger and coax another orgasm—a screaming one this time.

This is it. Inspired by her recent bed crawl, I arrange her in the doggy position and slide into her slick pussy from behind—and it's transcendent, like catching that perfect wave on a beautiful spring day. In fact, this feels too good—in that I'm on the verge of blowing my load already. Nope. I can't wipe out so quickly, not when the wave is this perfect. I grab Brooklyn's curvy little butt and thrust into her slower but deeper.

"Yes," she screams. "Yes!"

"Fuck..." Keeping the pace going, I lubricate my

index finger with some spit, then gently insert it into her butt.

She moans in pleasure.

I crook my finger just a smidge—which makes it so I can feel my cock going in and out of her.

"Evan!" she shouts as she comes, squeezing both my cock and my finger in the process, which pushes me over the edge. I grunt in pleasure as the most powerful orgasm of my life ignites my every nerve ending.

Afterward, I'm barely conscious, which is weird because I'm not usually the stereotypical guy who needs sleep right after sex.

Maybe the drowsiness is proportional to how much fun you've had? No idea, but all I have the energy for is to kiss Brooklyn and whisper, "That was amazing," before I'm out like a candle in a thunderstorm.

———

I wake up to the hungry grumbling of my stomach.

When I open my eyes, I see Brooklyn looking at me with an amused expression.

"That sounds like an emergency," she says. "If we don't feed you soon, you might go postal—or whatever the surfer equivalent is."

"Mental." I reach for the fancy phone on the nightstand and order us room service: a Japanese breakfast for me and a Croque Madame as well as a Raspberry Pain au Chocolat for Brooklyn, who seems to be in the mood for French cuisine.

As we do our morning toilette, I sneak glances at Brooklyn, who is still only half dressed.

A sunken feeling lodges somewhere in my stomach. After today, there will be two days left of her vacation, or really only one because the day after tomorrow she'll be flying to—

"Room service!" someone shouts at the top of their lungs.

Ah. Right. I toss on a robe and let the server in, then watch as he sets it all up by the pool on the balcony overlooking the ocean.

Another romantic meal will only worsen my malaise, but Brooklyn looks ecstatic when she joins me, and that makes me forget everything else.

During the scrumptious breakfast, we compare notes about our favorite classes back in middle school for some unknown reason, but the conversation only occupies a part of my attention as I keep marveling at one simple thing:

We've known each other for less than a week, yet I feel like I've known Brooklyn my whole life.

Chapter Twenty-One

BROOKLYN

I'm in trouble. I've grown to enjoy Evan's company too much. Case in point: the four-and-a-half-hour drive to Miami feels more like a fun road trip than a chore.

Before we reach our destination, Evan states that he wants to grab a quick lunch.

As we pull up to the place, I look it up online and frown. "This is a three-Michelin-star restaurant."

"That's why I picked it." Evan parks the car. "We don't have restaurants of this caliber in Palm Islet, so I want to take advantage of this opportunity while I can."

I look from my casual clothes to his. "I don't think we're dressed for it."

"It's lunchtime. They don't expect you to get fancy until dinner."

I sigh. "It also just sounds pricey."

He waves my words away. "Even if I spent a grand in fancy restaurants every day, it would still take two thousand seven hundred and forty years for me to run out of money."

I try to wrap my brain around that math and get a headache for my trouble. "Fine. Let's go."

He holds the door for me, and I step inside.

Yep. It looks amazing, like a restaurant version of the hotel we've just left. Our waitress, though, looks exactly like a poodle—a fact that makes me chuckle into my fist.

"What's so funny?" Evan asks when she leaves after seating us at the table.

I explain that I find it extra funny that our server looks like a poodle.

"Why?" he asks.

"When I think 'poodle,' I think 'French,' which is the cuisine here."

"French Bulldog sounds more French," Evan says. "But anyway, I was asking why you compare people to dog breeds."

I shrug. "Because I love dogs?"

Evan cocks his head in a very canine way. "What breed am I?"

I admit that his eyes remind me of a Siberian husky and his hair of a Golden Retriever.

"The latter makes sense," he says. "I am, after all, a Golden Retriever's dad."

He really is a good fur dad, and thinking of him in a fatherly role again tugs on something ineffable in my chest.

I do my best to shake it off. "By that logic, you

should resemble Sally in some way too, but that's not even remotely the case."

Actually, he is as good at licking body parts as a cat—especially my favorite body part named after a cat.

And now I'm blushing.

"That reminds me." Evan checks something on his phone, relaxes, and then looks back at me.

"What was that about?" I nod at the phone.

"I've been having Boone check on Harry and Sally," Evan explains. "So I just checked his latest report. He's already walked Harry, played with Sally, and fed them both."

Ah. He might just be a better fur father than I am a human mother because I haven't checked on Reagan at all today, let alone made sure that someone has fed him or played with him.

Feeling suddenly guilty, I excuse myself to go to the bathroom and call the camp from there.

A counselor who sounds like a child herself informs me that my son is too busy having fun to come to the phone, and that he's been thriving at the camp. "His only concern seems to be that he has to leave soon," she says in conclusion. "Have you thought about extending his stay?"

"I haven't," I lie. "But I will."

Hanging up, I sigh. It doesn't matter whether I "think about" extending Reagan's stay. Our tickets back are not the type you can change the date on. Nor would I want him to fly without me. Most importantly, I can't afford to pay for more camp.

When I get back, the food—a tasting course—is already waiting at the table.

As I swallow the escargot that is our first appetizer, I also swallow a moan of pleasure. My spirits lift instantly, in the same way as from a line of cocaine (I imagine). In fact, my eyes roll into the back of my head, and it's an effort to refocus them on Evan, who looks so smug you'd think he had hand-fed lettuce to these snails from child-hood and then cooked them personally.

"Good?" he asks.

"I didn't think French food could taste better than the breakfast this morning," I say. "But this is another level."

He nods. "That hotel's restaurant only has one Michelin star; this place has three."

Seems like despite his need for the simple life, when it comes to food, he's a billionaire at heart—hence the obsession with Michelin's guide. Speaking of... "Didn't that guide originate in France? I figure they'd be extra picky when it comes to their home cuisine."

"Maybe," he says. "I've always thought it was weird that the guide was published by a tire company."

I grin. "Why? Everyone knows that tire companies care about three things: the cost of rubber, the growth of the car market, and yummy food."

Evan's return grin is heart-fluttery. "I wonder if their guide is the reason the Michelin Man is so chubby."

I look at the tiny morsels on our plates. "I'm not sure if three-star restaurants are going to get anyone chubby. Oh, and I'm pretty sure the Michelin Man is made out of tires, but even if he weren't, it's not nice of you to fat-shame the poor mascot."

The Poodle shows up at that very moment, with two plates that have a ton more food on them compared to the first course.

Evan watches her leave suspiciously. "You mention small portion sizes, and they bring this out. What are the chances the chef is spying on us?"

"Maybe that's what separates one star from three stars." I spear a tiny piece of scallop and put it in my mouth. "Wow."

Not counting Vitamin D, this is the best thing I've had in my mouth in years.

We wolf down a few more courses, each better than the last, and when we're beyond stuffed, we head over to the Vizcaya Museum and Gardens, where we ignore the treasure hunt for a few minutes in favor of simply walking off the meal.

The place is insanely gorgeous and is by far the most romantic location I've ever been to. I don't know if it's the gardens, the art, or Evan's company, but I'm on the verge of swooning. And I'm not alone. About a dozen couples are here with us, using the location for their wedding photos.

Am I jealous of all the brides? No. Not at all. What would give anyone *that* idea?

"So..." I stop and look at Evan. "Any idea where the next clue might be?"

He shrugs. "I have no clue where the clue might be."

I purse my lips. "Why am I the only one who is taking this seriously?"

"Sorry," Evan says, but he sounds anything but.

"This is our last chance to find the clues," I remind him. "I say we comb through this place with a toothbrush."

"Right." Evan doesn't sound too thrilled.

Whatever. Since I'm motivated enough for the both of us, I seek the clues with everything I have, scanning all publicly available areas over and over while channeling my inner Robert Langdon.

Sadly, all my efforts amount to nothing, though I do manage to work up an appetite... for food, not Evan.

Fine, maybe both.

"Dinner?" Evan asks as if reading my thoughts.

"Sure." After that one appetite is satisfied, I'll see what I can do about the other.

———

As we eat at the self-proclaimed "best restaurant on South Beach," our conversation revolves around things that happened to us before we met, and it feels like we're both cramming for a final exam about the other.

The frantic get-to-know-you continues as we stroll on the nearby boardwalk, and I learn random things about Evan, like the fact that his favorite color is turquoise and his favorite texture is fleece. Whatever he tells me, I find fascinating, no matter how obscure or irrelevant-seeming—and that's bad. It highlights how deeply in trouble I am. Or more accurately, the trouble my heart is in.

I stop and very demonstratively glance at my tracker to check the time.

My dear Precious, typically at this late hour, I delight in the changes of your majestic brain waves as you move from one stage of beauty sleep to the next. Alas, today I have to resign myself to keeping watch on the scrumptious juices in your stomach and the delectable ones further south.

"It's getting a bit late to drive back," I say. Translation: "Let's get a room so I can have you inside me, now."

Evan glances at his watch. "I think you're right." He gestures at a fancy hotel nearby. "Let's go see if they have a room."

Translation: "I'm going to fuck you so hard you'll have trouble walking for the rest of your stay."

Clearly on the same wavelength, we jog over to the hotel, then sprint for the elevator once the Shih Tzu-like concierge hands Evan the keys.

Once in the room, we strip and race each other to another giant bed, but then things seem to slow down, and the way Evan takes me is unexpectedly slow and gentle. He stares deeply into my eyes when he enters me, and he interlaces his fingers with mine as we come together in a powerful release.

When it's all over and Evan wraps himself around me in a tight hug, I finally find the words to describe our sex session.

It was as though he was savoring his last moments with me.

Yeah. That's how I'm going to interpret it, and not use another two words that I dare not even think.

Love making.

Chapter Twenty-Two

EVAN

"I've got it!" someone shouts.

I open one eye.

Wearing only a hotel robe, Brooklyn is sitting on the bed cross-legged and pointing very pointedly at the treasure map, her hair disheveled and eyes wild —like those of a very sexy witch.

Of course. The stupid treasure map, I shouldn't have—

"It's the two saints." Brooklyn stabs at two points on the map, one after the other. "I can't believe I didn't think of it sooner."

I open both eyes.

"The four locations didn't *have* the clues—they *are* the clues," she says excitedly. "Or points on the map." She grabs a hotel pen and draws two lines on the map. "If you connect St. Petersburg and St. Augustine, the two cities with saints in the name, you get one line. If you also connect the two places that contain the M-girl names

Mia and Maria, the intersection between those two lines
has to be where the treasure is."

I sit on the bed and run a hand through my hair.
"Nice job. Can I make a phone call, brush my teeth, and
maybe eat before we head out?"

Brooklyn pouts like a child, but I head to the bathroom, close the door for privacy, and call Calvin. He
picks up right away and sounds amiable to the idea I
propose, so I tell him I owe him big and hang up. That
done, I brush my teeth.

When I come out, Brooklyn tells me she's already
ordered breakfast, which causes my stomach to rumble
gratefully.

———

During the breakfast and on the drive to our destination,
I regret initiating the cursed search for treasure. Without
it, we could do something more meaningful with our last
full day together—assuming today is that. Then again,
said hunt for treasure was what lured Brooklyn into
hanging out with me in the first place. I'm not sure she
would've done so without it.

I'm also not sure if I'm glad we got to spend all this
time together. Brooklyn is leaving tomorrow, and the
nearer that deadline gets, the heavier my chest grows.
Maybe it was also a mistake not putting any labels on our
relationship. Labels have warnings—at least on jars with
poison—and in this case, the warning should have been:
may develop feelings.

Then again, I had that conversation with Calvin, so maybe—

"Are we there yet?" Brooklyn asks, and I don't know if she's kidding, but she sounds just like a kid.

"A few more miles," I say.

"How do you know?" She looks around. "All I see is a forest."

I smile. "Then why would you ask if we're there yet?"

She shrugs.

"Our destination happens to *be* in the forest," I say. "At least according to this special app I used on my phone."

She narrows her eyes at me. "You didn't mention that earlier."

My smile widens. "I wasn't sure how you felt about hikes. Figured I'd better tell you once we're almost there."

She sighs theatrically. "If I had known about the hike, I would've brought different shoes."

"Hmm." I sneak a glance at her sneakers. "I think those should be fine. We can toss them into the washer after."

She scans rows and rows of trees passing by. "Maybe we'll get lucky, and there'll be a road leading to our destination?"

"If not a road, then maybe a trail, created by, say, a family of helpful bears."

"A hike and bears," she says. "Thanks for that."

We drive another twenty minutes until I declare a small clearing by the road to be a good parking spot.

"There *is* no road, is there?" Brooklyn asks. "Or even a bear trail."

I shake my head.

She gestures at a nearby private property sign. "Are we going to be trespassing during our hike?"

I face her. "If you want to go back, I understand."

"No." She sits straighter. "I'm seeing this thing through."

Chapter Twenty-Three

BROOKLYN

As it turns out, hiking in a Florida forest is as fun as working as a whipping boy (or girl), a leech collector (someone had to get them for the medieval doctors, right?), or a tax auditor. Thus far, I've walked into twenty spiderwebs and been hit by seven branches. All this has happened despite the fact that Evan has done the gentlemanly thing and taken the lead, and is therefore taking the brunt of these attacks onto himself.

And did I mention the humid heat? Or the horse-sized mosquitoes? Or the wild boar skeleton I almost stepped on? Or how Evan has saved my life four times now, catching me when I slipped? Or the blister forming on my right foot?

To put it another way: I should've given up when Evan gave me the chance by the car, but now we're too far into the hike for me to bail.

In my defense, the idea of a hike sounded kind of romantic. But I should've reminded myself that doing anything involving Evan sounds romantic, so why not do something while surrounded by civilization?

"I think that's it." Evan gestures at something dark in the distance.

At first, I think it's a big tree, but when we get a little closer, I realize it's a house—or a forest hut as they're probably called. No, this is a cabin... in the woods, a.k.a. the most common horror movie setting.

"Are you sure we should go in there?" I whisper. "We're trespassing already."

Evan glances at me. "You want to turn back?"

I slap at something trying to bite the back of my hand. "What are the chances your grandfather put the treasure in a serial killer's lair?"

How does Evan manage to raise his eyebrow in such a sexy manner? "Why a serial killer?"

I shrug. "I saw a special recently, and they said a lot of serial killers were native Floridians. Ted Bundy, Aileen Wuornos, David—"

"I don't see an ice cream truck anywhere," Evan says. "Or a guy dressed as a clown."

"You're thinking of John Wayne Gacy," I say. "And I don't think he was from the Sunshine State."

"Great, so we know there's no killer clown." Evan takes a confident step toward the cabin. "If you want, you can wait here."

"No way." But I do let him take the lead as he walks up to the structure and knocks.

No reply.

He pushes the door in.

There's no way that will just—

The door opens, and doesn't even creak or anything, which it would in a horror flick. Then again, maybe it was oiled with the fat of the killer's last victim?

"This is a bad idea," I whisper. "We're trespassing, and the door was unlocked—how sketch is that? Also—"

I'm not sure if Evan hears me, but he walks in.

I wait a beat but do not hear any screams of pain, so like an idiot, I follow... and gasp.

The place smells like pines and is surprisingly pretty cozy, with plush furniture and floors covered in furs and rugs. But that's not what I'm fascinated by. There's a literal treasure chest in the middle of the living room, one straight out of the set of *The Pirates of the Caribbean*.

Evan points at the chest. "I'm not as good as you when it comes to clues and whatnot, but I think that is what we've been searching for."

I have so many questions I don't even know where to start. What is this place? Who built it? Why? If this is the treasure, how did it survive all this time with the door unlocked?

Then again: We. Found. The. Treasure. I try not to jump up and down like Reagan would. "Can we just take it? What if it belongs to the serial killer?"

"When you dig up treasure, it's usually hidden on land that belongs to someone who isn't you, so you're talking about a generic issue with treasure hunting." Evan walks over to the chest and opens the lid.

Inside the chest is a smaller chest.

Evan mutters something and takes that smaller chest

out, only to find yet another, smaller chest nested inside, matryoshka style. Not surprisingly, there are more chests in it, and on and on until finally, Evan uncovers a glass box the size of his palm.

Inside this box is a very fancy men's watch but I barely look at it because all my attention is captured by the most beautiful pair of earrings I've ever seen, in real life and in movies. Each piece is made out of white gold or platinum and prominently features a giant sapphire that reminds me of the necklace the old lady dropped into the ocean in *Titanic*.

"Can I call dibs on the watch?" Evan asks.

I drag my eyes away from the earrings. "Why? All of it belongs to you... or to the serial killer."

Evan shakes his head. "A deal's a deal. We agreed to share the treasure." With that, he takes the watch and clips it on his wrist.

Given that we're in a cabin in the woods, how likely is it that I'm possessed by the ghost of a crow? My eyes leap back to the shiny earrings just as I mutter, "This isn't right. These look like they cost a fortune."

Evan shrugs. "They belonged to my late grand-mother. Having gotten to know you, I'm confident she would want you to have them."

I shouldn't accept something this expensive, let alone a family heirloom. It's way too much. All I did to earn this was take Evan on what was basically a fun excursion around Florida. But the earrings are so freaking beautiful. And Evan is a billionaire, so the cost means nothing to him, right? Not to mention—

No. I'm just rationalizing. I can't in good conscience—

"Just try them on," Evan murmurs.

I take a step back. "If I put them on, I'm not sure I'll be able to give them back."

"I won't take them back," Evan says. "They either stay here or come with us."

"Leaving these earrings here in the middle of nowhere would be sacrilege." Heart hammering in my chest, I put the earrings on.

"Gorgeous," Evan says, studying me with a lopsided smile. "Now, let's go."

"Wait." I take out my phone, switch to selfie mode, and look at myself.

Wow. I'm not usually into jewelry, but the flood of warm feelings toward the earrings makes me worried I might turn evil, develop multiple personality disorder, and then spend all my days calling the earrings "my preciouses" in a voice not unlike that of Gollum's.

"Ready?" Evan asks.

I nod, and he leads the way back to the car, a trip that passes with a lot more ease than our trek here—for which I credit "my preciouses," of course.

As we drive back, I admire myself in the mirror on the sun visor. Then, as we pull into Evan's driveway, I look at his watch, really noticing it for the first time.

I frown. "Your watch looks familiar."

Evan parks the car and looks at his wrist. "It was my grandfather's. He never let anyone touch it."

Hold on. "Never?"

"No. He was pretty frugal, especially considering his wealth, but—"

"You're lying." The car suddenly feels suffocating, so I get out.

Evan leaps out of the car as well. "Why did you say that?"

Given how guilty he looks as he asks, I'm pretty sure that I'm right, even if I'm confused as to his motives.

"I saw that exact watch on your wrist in the photo album," I say. "You wore a suit, and your grandfather was in that same picture. If he was so against anyone touching his watch, why was he so happy on that occasion?"

I've never seen someone literally smack themselves on the forehead, but that is what Evan does. "I completely forgot about that picture."

I put my hands on my hips. "Explain."

Evan sighs. "Any chance we can discuss this over dinner?"

"No. Tell me now." I've suddenly lost my appetite.

Evan expels a breath. "You've probably already guessed it. The treasure hunt was a farce."

I gape at him. "What?"

I knew he was lying, and that hurt, but I hadn't yet made *that* big of a leap.

Evan takes a step back. "Shit. If you didn't guess it, I guess I've just spilled it."

"The treasure hunt wasn't real?" I demand.

Now that I think about it, that explains a lot of little peculiarities. Like how comfortable Evan was back at the cabin in the woods. He probably owns that place. Or how the first clue was the college he went to. Or how he wasn't ever disappointed or surprised when we didn't find any clues at the "wrong" locations. He didn't not care because he was *that* rich; it was—

"Remember when I offered to show you around?" Evan asks defensively. "You refused and then mentioned that you liked treasure maps, so I made up a story about my grandfather leaving one for me."

I just stare open-mouthed, so he continues. "I created the map and the code using Florida history and aged it with coffee stains."

So that's why the documents smelled of something that reminded me of NYC—it was the coffee.

"I then asked Boone to place the watch and the earrings in a box at the old cabin. The nesting chests were his touch—let's hope he didn't pick them up at the junkyard."

I grit my teeth. "The cabin in the woods was yours, wasn't it?"

He nods. "It and a few acres of the surrounding forest. We weren't trespassing. Sorry that I led you to believe that we were."

"You're sorry," I say hollowly.

"Yes," he says. "Sorry that I lied. I simply wanted to spend some time with you."

Oh.

Now I don't know what to think or feel. Should I be mad? Flattered? Both? I think both, right? Then again, the treasure hunt was fun and I got to spend all that time in his company, which was beyond fun, so maybe I should be grateful?

Yeah, this is beyond confusing, especially given that I'm flying home tomorrow and feel like an elephant has taken a dump on my chest each time I think about getting on that plane.

Evan takes a step toward me. "Let's go inside. I'll make dinner and—"

"No." I wipe a bead of sweat off my brow. "I need time to process all of this."

Evan's face falls. "Time is the one thing we don't have."

The stupid elephant takes another shit. "I know that." It's part of the reason I'm so overwhelmed.

Evan closes the distance between us and takes my hand, scrambling my already-jumbled brain. "There was something I wanted to talk to you about over dinner."

My belly flutters, like strips of paper caught in the wind. "What?"

He squeezes my hand. "I don't want you to leave."

My skin tingles, and not just where his hand touches mine. As soon as I hear those words, I realize that it's been my biggest dream to hear him say them—because I so desperately want to stay. Except maybe I should've dreaded these words instead. They will make leaving that much harder, and staying isn't an option. "You don't?" I manage to say.

He shakes his head vehemently.

I stare into the depths of his Husky-blue eyes. "I don't want to leave either, but I have to." "Understatement" isn't just a word that would score me seventeen points in Scrabble.

"But do you?" he asks, frowning.

I cover his hand with mine. "I live in New York, and you live here."

"That can be changed," he says. "I know it's only been a few days, but I thought that maybe—"

"Stop," I say breathlessly. "This was supposed to be a fling." Which happened despite our better judgements.

"No." He tenderly massages my palm. "I didn't want to label whatever it was precisely because I hated the idea of a fling. And so did you."

My heartbeat skyrockets. "Are you going to New York with me?" Scratch my earlier dream. This is it.

He frowns. "I own a lot of land here, which comes with responsibilities. Also, I can't just leave my volunteering gig. And there's the surfing." He looks at me imploringly. "I was hoping I could persuade you to stay here."

And there it goes, my dream bursting like a balloon inside a papier-mâché head. I slowly blink at Evan, like Sally might. "I can't stay."

"Why not?" He pulls his hands away, and I miss them immediately.

"My job is—"

"Remember the call I had to make this morning?" Evan asks, his eyes gleaming. "It was to talk to Calvin."

I stare at him. "Calvin being the guy with the pet cows?"

"Exactly, though he's more famous around these

parts for being the owner of the local veterinary clinic—
the cows and his other furry charges are an extension of
that. In any case, he said he would let you groom the dogs
in his practice and pay—"

"No." I swallow. "Even if I had a job—and that one
sounds too good to be true—I couldn't stay."

He stiffens, and not in a fun way. "No?"

"My whole life is in Brooklyn." Maybe I should make
"understatement" my middle name?

He exhales, loudly. "Then don't stay. Extend your
vacation for a month. See where this goes. Maybe then I
could—"

"I can't."

Even though I desperately want to, more than
anything, it's just not possible.

"You can't, or you don't want to?" The question is
asked with such intensity that I take a step back.

"Believe me, I'd love to extend the vacation, but I
really can't. There's something I never told you,
something—"

"You have someone in New York? A boyfriend?" His
blue gaze turns icy. "A husband?"

"No!" How could he think that of me? I gather my
courage. I should've come clean earlier, many times over.
"I'm single," I say and take a breath. "But I do have a son,
and he can't just—"

"A son?" Evan looks dazed, like he's just smoked
enough weed to kill Cheech and Chong.

"Yes. I'm sorry I never mentioned him." Despite a
million opportunities to do so. "I know I should have,

but this was temporary, and you hate children, so I just—"

"Hate children?" Evan's gaze approaches the coldness of absolute zero. "That's your shitty excuse for lying?"

My whole body tenses. The accusation hurts all the more because it's not completely unfair, but has he not heard the proverb about glass houses? "Unlike you with your treasure bullshit, I didn't lie."

I simply omitted a little bit of the truth.

"Then what word would you use?" he says in a tone I do not appreciate. "You didn't tell me about the most important thing in your life. I thought I knew you, but I'm not so sure anymore."

I grit my teeth. "I thought you weren't a lying asshole, but maybe I didn't know you that well either."

He turns from me. "I'd better go before I say something I'll regret."

"Wait." I reach for my earlobes.

He turns back, and it could be my imagination, but I glimpse a spark of hope in his eyes.

I unclasp the earrings. "I don't feel right taking these. Not after—"

"Then toss them into the garbage," he snaps before he turns away again and strides into his house, slamming the door so hard behind him that I'm pretty sure he'll need new hinges.

Feeling just like those hinges, I stand there, fighting the urge to run after him. To bang on the door until he opens it, then slant my lips over his and claim one more night. The last night.

But no.

More time with him will just make me hurt all the more. In a way, this fight was a blessing in disguise. We were going to be forced apart anyway, but this made it like ripping off a Band-Aid. Except I feel more like I'm a yeti who is getting a full-body wax.

With a monumental effort, I force my legs to walk toward the rental, all the while ignoring the pressure building behind my eyes.

Once inside, I get ready for bed, even though it's not even dusk yet. It's not until I step into the shower that a sob escapes my lips, my tears mixing with the warm water pelting my skin.

Chapter Twenty-Four

EVAN

In my house, I slam door after door, and only stop when Harry looks at me worriedly and whines.

Human dude, this is not awesome at all. I've never seen you so unchill.

Sally seems concerned also, if the nervous swish of her tail is anything to judge by.

We thought we had an understanding with our captor: everyone must act civilized, or some of us will eat the other's eyeballs.

"Sorry, guys." I stomp over to the kitchen and feed them before I fix myself my favorite grilled Brie sandwich —which today tastes like sugar-free, fat-free, non-dairy, freeze-dried astronaut ice cream.

Midway through the meal, I push my plate away, set my laptop on the kitchen table next to a shot glass, and rummage in my freezer for a frosty bottle of St. Augustine vodka.

Now that all is ready, I video call Mason.

As soon as he picks up, I ask, "Drink with me?".

He cocks his head. "Where's the obligatory, 'Hey, Mason, how's it going?'"

I sigh. "Hey, Mason, how's it fucking going? Now, can we drink?"

Nodding, Mason disappears, then reappears with a gold bottle adorned with a double-headed eagle.

I pick up my shot glass. "The million-dollar vodka, again?"

"One point three million." Mason pours himself an 81,250-dollar shot. "Inflation is a bitch."

I down my shot in one gulp and follow with another.

When I look at the screen, Mason's eyebrow is arched. "Are things *that* bad?"

"I don't want to talk about it." I down another shot.

"Good." Mason matches my shot with his.

"Fine." Another shot. "I'll tell you if you tell me why you called the other day."

"We lost a game," Mason says. "And I don't see the point of you telling me anything."

So I was right when I theorized about his hockey team losing the other day. Not that being right—or anything else—can cheer me up at the moment.

"It started when a woman rented my Airbnb," I say and launch into the story, taking shots at critical points as I go. Throughout my whole tale, Mason's expression doesn't change, and he's silent when I finish.

"Gee. Thanks for the advice." I take another shot.

"You know I don't do relationships." Mason pours himself more vodka. "What good is my advice?"

"I didn't think I did relationships either."

"And that was smart. Go back to that. Don't surfers have something like puck bunnies?"

I shake my head. "Professional surfers have groupies. Beach bunnies are what some people call female surfers, but I'm sure that's not what you mean."

"Thanks for expanding my vocabulary," Mason says. "It should come in handy during my next game of Scrabble."

"Fuck you." I knew I shouldn't have told him about my fondness for that game.

I demonstratively reach to turn off my phone.

"Wait." Mason throws back his shot. "Don't you think you overreacted when she told you about her son?"

"Next question," I growl.

"Fine. Why can't the two of you have a long-distance relationship?"

"Long-distance?" I scratch the back of my head. "Honestly, I didn't even think about that."

"Not with your head, that's for sure."

I shrug. "What would be the point of a long-distance relationship?"

"What is the point of *any* relationship?"

I have no clue, but I do know that I want Brooklyn physically next to me, not as a little picture on a screen. "This conversation is getting tedious."

Mason spreads his hands. "I told you that I didn't see the point of you telling me anything."

He did, and he hasn't been useful in the slightest, but

somehow, I feel a tiny bit better. Enough to stop drinking, anyway.

"Thanks," I tell Mason. "I think I'll go lie down."

"Lightweight."

"Compared to a bear like you, everyone is a fucking lightweight." Am I officially drunk, or was that a good comeback?

I have no idea, but I think Mason smirks before he hangs up.

Pushing the vodka bottle away, I notice how much is gone.

Shit.

I get to my feet, and the stupid room starts spinning.

This is what happens when you talk about your feelings. I hope I don't have alcohol poisoning.

It's a good thing I fed Harry and Sally. I can't do shit now. The best I can hope for is to make it to my bed.

———

I wake up on the couch in the living room.

Huh. Guess my ambitious post-drinking journey to the bedroom didn't pan out as I hoped. Then again, I should have a splitting headache, but I don't. Just a wooziness and lack of desire to drink ever again.

Maybe I should call Mason and tell him I'm not such a lightweight after all?

Speaking of that conversation, now that I'm sober (or at least soberer), I realize Mason was right when he accused me of overreacting to the news of Brooklyn having a son. I would've reached that conclusion myself, I'm sure, but I guess it's helpful to have it pointed out. I did overreact, and I suspect it was partly because Brooklyn happened to say "you hate children," a phrase I've heard a bunch of times during breakups, usually after I share about my vasectomy.

I don't hate children. If I did, why would I volunteer at the camp? I got a vasectomy for a different reason altogether.

Speaking of the cursed vasectomy, I never told Brooklyn about that, which might be as much of a lie of omission as her not telling me about her son. And let's not forget, I did lie to her about the treasure, which she took rather well.

Fuck. What right did I have to get so pissed off? No idea, but I bet being hangry was a variable yet again.

I have to fix this.

Leaping to my feet, I sprint to the bathroom and make myself presentable before hurrying over to Brooklyn's rental—which is empty.

Well, not completely empty. On the kitchen table is a note with my grandmother's earrings on it.

I couldn't throw them out, and I can't take them with me, it says.

Shit. She checked out. Just like that. No goodbye?

I guess I don't deserve one after almost biting her head off.

Sticking the earrings into my pocket, I call Boone.

"Howdy," Boone says.

"Morning. I need a ride."

This time, I'm not just giving Boone a chance to make money. In our tiny town, waiting for an Uber would take too long.

Chasing her down at the airport might be cliché, but it's the only move I have left.

"Morning?" I can hear a grin in Boone's voice. "It's twelve-thirty in the afternoon."

Fuck. According to the clock on the microwave, he's right.

This might be why I don't feel particularly hungover, which still doesn't mean my BAC is under .08, which would make me safe to drive.

When is Brooklyn's flight? Did I miss it already?

Fuck. I don't even know which airport or airline. I was counting on convincing her to stay so much that I never asked for the specifics of her trip home.

"When can you be here?" I demand.

"Two minutes," Boone says. "I was just cutting the grass in your community."

Ah. Right. Hiring him despite his prior conviction was one of the few things I strongarmed the HOA to do. Boone got into trouble with the law for making home-made moonshine without a license, which doesn't exactly scream "incapable of doing landscaping."

I run back to my place and grab some food from the fridge—it's best I talk to Brooklyn on a full stomach, assuming I get the chance. While I'm here, I feed Harry and Sally as well, and by the time I'm done, Boone is pulling into my driveway.

"To the Jacksonville Airport," I tell him, choosing

the closest and biggest one as it's most likely to be Brooklyn's point of departure. "And punch it."

He does just that, driving like he's in an episode of *The Dukes of Hazzard*.

As we go, I use my phone to research which flight Brooklyn is likely to be on, and staring at a screen in such a fast-moving car doesn't help my remaining wooziness. I ignore flights before one p.m., as I have no chance of making it to those, and focus on the ones headed to JFK because it's closest to Brooklyn. That gives me one candidate: the Delta flight at one-thirty.

Except even with our current speed, I won't be able to reach the airport in time to intercept her if she's on it. When I tell that to Boone, he *really* floors the gas. His poor car shakes as if it's going to fall apart, but miraculously, it doesn't.

Equally miraculously, we don't get stopped by the police. Instead, we enter the airport at such a speed that Boone almost runs over an old lady before he comes to a screeching halt—a New Yorker lady, I suspect, at least if the bird she flips us is anything to go by.

As I hop out of the car, Boone wishes me luck, his labored breathing sounding like he's carried me here on his back.

I sprint inside and dash for the nearest ticket booth. By now, Brooklyn must be through security, and they won't let me through if I'm not a passenger.

"Give me a ticket," I demand.

The lady at the counter frowns. "Where to?"

"YUM," I reply. I've never flown to this particular

airport in Yuma, Arizona, but with a code like that, they'd better have the best restaurants in the world.

The lady hands me the ticket and I run for security, thanking the TSA gods I'm precleared for expedited screening.

The problem is, there's a line of other expedited passengers, and it's long—though not as long as the regular line.

Gritting my teeth, I wait. And wait. And wait.

By the time I'm through security, I have to run at full speed to Brooklyn's gate.

Shit. They're almost done boarding, and what's worse, I see Brooklyn showing the agent her ticket.

I guessed right about her flight. And I'm still going to miss it.

"Wait!" I shout. "Brooklyn, hold up!"

No reaction—other than walking into the gate. She didn't hear me or, worse, pretended not to hear.

Fuck.

I pick up speed, but they're already closing the doors.

By the time I get there, the doors are locked and the agent who locked them is walking away.

I run after her. "Can I get on there, please?" I jab my thumb at the gate, not bothering to mention that I'm not a passenger.

"I'm sorry, hon," she says. "Once that door is closed, it can't be opened. You'll have to catch the next flight."

I pull out a pile of hundreds from my wallet. "Can you make an exception, just this once?"

The agent greedily eyes the cash. "Trust me, for that, if I could, I would. But I can't."

And that's that.

I'm not sure if it's the post-chase slump or the hangover, but I find myself sinking into a nearby chair, utterly drained and defeated.

Maybe it's for the best.

Even if I'd caught up with Brooklyn, I have no idea what I would've said.

Chapter Twenty-Five

BROOKLYN

"What took you so long?" Reagan asks me when I get to my seat.

"I have a better question: why didn't you wait for me?" I say sternly.

As soon as I showed my son's ticket to the agent, he beelined for his seat, sneaking by other passengers and climbing over empty seats.

"I didn't wait because you take too long." Reagan beams me the boyish grin that lets him get away with almost anything.

The bright side of his charm and skills in prevarication—he might become a lawyer someday. Or is that the dark side?

"Your attention, please," says a disembodied voice.

As the safety spiel goes on, I once again doubt the whole "put the oxygen mask on yourself before your child" bit because it goes against every one of my maternal instincts.

"The camp was so awesome," Reagan says when the safety announcement is over. "We went hiking and ate s'mores and—"

He proceeds to excitedly describe his experience, and I listen intently until the plane lifts off, at which point I only pay half attention because as Florida gets smaller and smaller in the window, something in my chest constricts in direct proportion.

Crap. I had hoped that the farther I got from Evan, the better I would feel. So far, it seems like the opposite is true, and although hearing Reagan excitedly share his camp adventures cheers me up somewhat, it also reminds me of things Evan and I did, like hiking and eating yummy meals. Also, the nearby happily married couple reminds me of Evan too, and I feel an illogical twinge of jealousy that they get to be together while Evan and I are about to be separated by hundreds of miles after ending things on such bad terms.

It takes a huge effort to keep up a happy façade for my son, so much so that when we get home and I'm alone in my bed, I end up crying extra loudly into my pillow, like a baby banshee.

Chapter Twenty-Six

BROOKLYN

"'Time heals all wounds' is total bullshit," I say as I lather Mr. Goobers with shampoo.

Jolene and Dorothy nod in unison, urging me to keep talking.

I check on Reagan, who is still helping out at the other end of the salon and not causing mischief. Today is our first "bring your son to work day," and I don't want it to be our last.

"It's been ninety-six hours since I left Florida," I continue. "But I'm missing Evan more, not less."

Jolene and Dorothy nod again.

"It doesn't help that he called me." I sigh. "And texted me, and even wrote a message to me on the Airbnb app."

"I saw the review he left there," Jolene says. "Five stars of 'just take my call, please.'"

I check to see if I'm happy with how sudsy Mr. Goobers is. Because he's a Komondor, he looks like a mop on a regular day, but with foam in the picture, even an experienced janitor might grab him by mistake and start mopping away.

"Maybe you should take his call?" Dorothy suggests softly.

I start rinsing Mr. Goobers. "As soon as I decided I would, he stopped calling."

"When was that?" Jolene demands.

I shrug. "A few hours ago?"

"So how about you call him back?" Dorothy suggests.

"I'm not there yet." But I'm getting close to it. "But enough about me. What's new with you guys?"

Dorothy exchanges a shy glance with Jolene, who nods minutely.

Dorothy takes a deep breath. "We're dating."

"And we've wanted to tell you for a while," Jolene says. "But it never quite came up."

"You are?" And I'm not jealous at all, I swear on a pack of Bibles. "Who?"

They exchange a confused glance. "Dorothy just told you," Jolene says. "We're dating... each other."

I stare at my friends unblinkingly. "You're dating. As in romantically?" It was hard to believe they'd collaborated together enough to get me that vacation, but this—

"What can I say?" Jolene shrugs. "Opposites attract."

"How are we opposites?" Dorothy demands.

"Sexually," Jolene says without a moment of hesitation. "Also spiritually, temperament—"

"Wait." I turn to Dorothy. "You're gay?"

Dorothy blushes. "Consider this me coming out."

I turn to Jolene. "But... all you do is talk about dicks." Also, though I won't bring it up, I've seen her leave a bar with a dude more than once.

Jolene grins. "Didn't I tell you I was pansexual?"

"No."

She frowns. "I could swear that I did."

Did she? "You talk about something-sexual so much I sometimes tune you out."

"And you're not alone," Dorothy adds.

"People not listening isn't my problem," Jolene says. "All I know is that I've always been open about it. I'm attracted to people regardless of their gender... but you're right about one thing. I do like dicks, which is why I bought one of the best ones for Dorothy to use."

Shit. This does explain the way they've been together lately. Case in point: Dorothy came with Jolene today to pamper Jolene's dog, something that never would've happened in the past. But—

"You promised to be discrete," Dorothy hisses, bringing me out of my revelatory daze.

"I didn't mention which of my orifices Toto penetrated," Jolene counters. "Isn't that the definition of being discrete?"

They start to argue, and the avalanche of TMI continues, but I'm still too stunned to say anything... that is, until I blurt, "If you two break up, I'm staying friends with both of you and not choosing sides. Ever. I don't care who does what and to whom. Got it?"

"Fair," they say in unison.

"But I don't think we will break up," Dorothy adds shyly. "Even if we do occasionally fight."

Occasionally?

To my shock, Jolene grabs Dorothy's hand and squeezes it tenderly. "I don't think we'll break up either. But even if we do, we'll get back together—the makeup sex will be that good."

That's it. Mind officially blown. If this were the first of April, I'd suspect this to be a prank, but I can tell that it's not—the tender glance they just shared can't be faked. At least these two are not that good at acting.

"I'm happy for you guys," I say when I realize Jolene is looking at me expectantly, and Dorothy with a tinge of worry. "I really, truly am."

"Thank you," Dorothy says.

"Yeah," Jolene says. "And I'm sure you and Evan will—"

The salon door opens with a loud chime, and I gape as Evan walks in, looking as dashing as ever.

Wait. Am I hallucinating him because Jolene just said his name? Or is it some weird doppelganger?

Nope.

This is him.

There's no mistaking those Husky eyes and broad shoulders.

Butterflies start an orgy in my belly.

"That's him," I whisper to my friends, still stunned.

They turn in unison, and Jolene whistles, then whispers, "Is he the devil? I spoke his name, and there he is."

"Neveah!" Dorothy yells. "Can you take over here?"

I shake my head but keep my eyes on Evan, who is scanning the place, clearly seeking me out. "Neveah will make Mr. Goobers look like a poodle."

"So what?" Dorothy says. "Anything will be an improvement over his current Cousin Itt cosplay."

"I bet Mr. Goobers will look amazeballs with a poodle 'do," Jolene says. "All the bitches will be at his feet."

It's possible Jolene says more, but Evan spots me in that moment and strides my way, so I dazedly step toward him, leaving the dog and my friends behind.

What I really want is to jump on Evan and climb him like a tree, but I still don't know where he and I stand. Plus my boss is at the register and my friends are behind me—not to mention my son is in the corner. So I have to come up with something tamer, like a weak, "Hi."

"Hi," Evan replies softly when he's a few feet from me. "I—"

"Mr. Wilcox?" Reagan exclaims.

My feet are suddenly glued to the floor, my eyes bulging.

When Evan spots my son, he halts in his tracks, and I can tell he wants to rub his eyes, to check if he's dreaming.

"Hey, kid," he says instead. "I've already told you: call me Evan."

"Hold up," I exclaim, way too loudly. "How do you two know each other?"

Am I being punked? Are there reality TV cameras around?

First, my friends have become a couple. Now my son and my I-don't-yet-know-what-to-call-him know each other?

Reagan frowns at me. "Mr. Evan is the surfing instructor at the camp. I told you all about him on the plane."

What is it with everyone chastising me for not listening? To be fair, I *was* only half listening on the plane. Of course, I don't know if "Mr. Wilcox" would've even registered as "Evan" if I'd been paying full attention.

"Hold on a minute." Evan's gaze ping-pongs between Reagan and me. "Reagan is your son?" He turns to Reagan. "Brooklyn is your mom?"

Reagan looks at him with his own super-confused expression. "How do you two know each other?"

How do I answer that without using words like "vacation fling," "hookup," and "orgasms?" I've never brought a guy home or even talked to Reagan about the possibility of my dating someone, so this is completely new territory for me. How would he react if he learned that his "Mr. Evan" and I have been engaged in something with no labels? Not to mention, we still are in the "no label" territory, as I have no idea what Evan is doing here.

"Your mom was my neighbor during her vacation," Evan says, and I'm so grateful I could kiss him. Except that would shock Reagan even more, so I just nod and throw my friends a pleading look.

"Ice cream," Jolene says immediately. "Who wants to go get some?"

Mr. Goobers wags his tail for all his shaggy fur is worth.

"Not you." Jolene wipes off the soap his tail sprayed her way. "You're getting poodled. But I will give you peanut butter when we get home."

Reagan looks at me pleadingly. "Can I go too?"

"Sure, but I have to stay here, so it will just be with Aunts Dorothy and Jolene," I say magnanimously.

"Okay." Reagan grins. "Can I have five scoops?"

It's like he knows he's got leverage. "Four, but not chocolate, tiramisu, or any other flavor that has caffeine in it." This last bit is more for my friends' benefit than Reagan's.

"Deal," Reagan says eagerly, making me think his first offer was a negotiating tactic for four scoops all along.

Definitely a lawyer to be.

"Let's go." Jolene grabs Reagan's right hand and Dorothy his left—and he lets them. If I'd done it, he'd stomp his foot and remind me that he's not a little kid anymore.

Just as they're about to walk out, Reagan turns to me and grins mischievously. "Bye, Mom. Have fun talking to your *boyfriend*."

My mouth falls open, and I want to sink through the floor. It doesn't help that Jolene cackles like an evil villain, and Dorothy snorts like a horny deer.

Fortunately, the two of them get my son out of the salon before I have to think of a reply.

When the door closes, it occurs to me that if I can get past the embarrassment of what has just happened, there is a bright side. The way Reagan called Evan my boyfriend was so casually teasing that it's unlikely he minds the idea of us dating. Maybe he even approves of it.

Not that we're dating. We're still in the no-labels territory. Or worse, broken up. Except... he's here.

Why is he here?

Before I can ask, Evan closes the remaining distance between us. "I still can't believe it," he says, shaking his head. "Reagan was my favorite student at the camp, and he's your son."

I rub my throbbing temples. "Don't try to change the subject."

Evan blinks at me. "What subject?"

Ah. Right. Just because I'm thinking a question so loudly in my head doesn't mean that Evan can hear it. "What are you doing here?"

"Hold that thought." Evan walks over to my boss, says something I can't hear, then pulls out his wallet and hands over a few bills. Returning, he gestures at the door. "Let's go."

It's my turn to blink. "What did you do?"

"Paid for a private grooming session."

For a dog or for himself? "I didn't think we did those."

Evan shrugs. "You do when the price is right."

Okay. I follow him out of the salon, and we cross the street to a small wooded patch that passes for a park in this neighborhood. I take a seat on the bench where I usually eat lunch, and Evan joins me.

I stare at him expectantly.

He takes a breath. "I'm sorry," he says softly, his eyes matching the clear sky above as he gazes at me.

I dampen my lips. "Oh?"

He takes my hand in his. "I'm sorry about the way I acted when you told me about Reagan. You had every right not to share all the details of your life with me and—"

"No." I swallow. "I should've told you. I wanted to tell you. I just—"

"It's okay." He squeezes my hand. "I also want to make something clear: I don't dislike kids. Not at all. I never would have volunteered at the camp if that were the case. Also, as it turns out, your kid is particularly likeable."

He totally is—though I'm admittedly biased. "Now I feel even worse about what I said about you."

Evan waves it off. "You saw me with a mangled Pikachu in my hand, and I said something about some brat. It wasn't a completely unreasonable accusation. It just hurt to hear it after we'd gotten to know each other. Plus, you're not the first woman to say it to me."

I frown. "I'm not?"

Evan releases my hand. "There's something I should've told you as well. Something private."

My heart sinks. Is Evan about to tell me he's married? Engaged? I brace myself for the worst.

"I had a vasectomy," he says, as if admitting something shameful.

That's not at all what I expected him to say. A vasectomy? When? Why?

"Women would always break up with me after I told them about it," Evan continues. "Which is why I didn't tell you. I wanted to, and I was going to, soon, but—"

"You thought I would break up with you. Like the others," I say, staring at him.

"Will you?"

Does that mean we aren't already broken up? And what about the whole no-labels thing?

"I won't," I say firmly. Because whatever we call or don't call this thing between us, his vasectomy is definitely not a problem for me.

"Because you already have a son?" he asks, his face brightening.

"That, and because..." I swallow the sudden lump in my throat. "I can't have any more kids."

Evan's eyes widen. "Oh. Are you—"

"Remember my dislike of hospitals because I almost died in one?"

He nods.

"That was when I was giving birth to Reagan." I take in a deep breath and wipe away the dust that's gotten into my eyes for some reason. "After saving me, the surgeon told me that I'm unlikely to ever get pregnant naturally again."

Evan grabs my hand again and gives it a gentle squeeze. "I'm so sorry."

"It's fine." I feel especially fine when he holds my hand the way he does. "If I desperately want another kid in the future, there are options like IVF." It's extremely expensive, but everything medical is. "Can I ask why you got the vasectomy?"

As soon as I see the pain in his eyes, I regret the intrusive question, but it's too late.

"I was grieving for my mother at the time," he says. "It's possible I should've held off on that decision until later. The thing is, I learned that if I ever had a female child, it would be a near certainty that she'd end up like my mom. I couldn't imagine that kind of pain, so I went out and got myself the best birth control available."

I gasp and then envelop him in a tight hug, fighting tears the whole time. "That really sucks. I'm sorry."

"Thanks," he says huskily when I pull away. "Like you, I could have a child if I *really* wanted one. A vasectomy can sometimes be reversed, and there's always sperm retrieval." He shudders a little as he says that last bit. "It's also possible to screen an embryo's DNA."

I nod, and we stare at each other for a long moment. I fight the urge to hug him more, or worse, kiss him. I fight it because he still hasn't told me one very important thing.

"So..." I clear my throat. "Why are you here?"

I can sort of guess, but I want to hear him say it.

The pain fades from his gaze, replaced by a heated intensity that gives the butterflies in my belly a second wind. Uncorking fresh bottles of lube, they resume their orgy as Evan tucks a tuft of hair behind my ear. "I decided it's time for me to come to New York for a vacation," he says with a crooked grin.

"A vacation?" Maybe it's not an orgy the butterflies are having, but a gangbang?

"One that will last until we figure out whatever it is that's going on between us," he confirms.

So... my guess was right. It makes me want to pump my fist in the air and have my way with Evan right here on this bench, for all the aggressive pigeons to see. "And what if it takes a while?"

"I'll be here as long as it takes." He scoots closer to me on the bench—and we were already pretty cozy.

My heart further picks up pace. "But what about your real estate?" Has he always radiated this much warmth? It's like he's brought the Florida sun with him.

"I listed my house on Airbnb and hired someone to manage it all," he says.

"And the camp?" Why am I not kissing him already?

His forehead wrinkles. "Vic owed me a favor, so I asked him to take over for me at the camp."

"Dr. Hugo surfs?" Why am I still misusing our lips by talking?

As if reading my mind, Evan examines my lips hungrily. "The class will feature kayaking for the time being."

"What about your own surfing?" My nipples are uncomfortably hard against my shirt, so I readjust my bra.

Evan's eyes heat up—he's clearly noticed my ladylike behavior. "Rockaway Beach in Queens is apparently a great surfing spot... though I would have come to you even if you lived in the desert."

"You would have?" I breathe, my chest constricting.

"Yes." He cradles my face with his big, warm hands. "I realized something. You hold the treasure map to my heart."

The butterflies in my belly reach a simultaneous orgasm. "Hey, that's my thing."

"Then let me put it another way." He leans in until our lips brush, and I can smell the faint mintiness of his breath. "I love you," he whispers. "I know we haven't known each other for that long, but I—"

"I love you too." I lay my hands over his and stare into his eyes. "You're like the perfect wave I've always wanted to ride."

"Hey, that's my thing," he breathes, and his lips finally clash with mine.

The kiss is scorching and deep. It feels like the combined total of all the kisses we would've had if I had stayed. We reaffirm in our dancing tongues all the love we've just admitted to each other and make promises of a bright future, one that I'm all too excited to begin.

Epilogue

BROOKLYN

"I can't believe you're a farm girl now," Jolene says, gesturing at the sheep in the distance.

I look around and view my new home from her perspective—the groves with the fruit trees, the fields of grains, all the fluffy livestock, and most importantly, the ocean surf in the distance.

Yep. Sometimes I pinch myself to make sure this is my life. Until Evan set this whole thing up, I didn't even think beachfront farms were a thing, but it turns out they are. You just have to make sure the soil is fertile, but that's something you need to do on any farm. There are challenges, for sure, like the equipment corroding faster because of the ocean air, but there are benefits as well, like fewer pests, which makes it easier to keep our food organic.

"What I can't believe is that she agreed to become a Floridian," Dorothy says. "There's no good pizza anywhere in sight, and no landmarks."

Evan makes a killer pizza, and St. Augustine has plenty of landmarks, but I don't want to argue. "Couldn't help it," I say instead. "After the wedding, Reagan teamed up with Evan until they chipped away at every argument I could come up with against moving."

Not that I minded the move at all, but my friends are such ardent New Yorkers that I have to at least pretend that I put up a fight.

"Well, you shouldn't have had the wedding in Florida," Jolene says sagely. "Or sent Reagan to that camp again."

She's right. Between the wedding and all that time at the camp, Reagan fell madly in love with the Sunshine State. "In my defense, I *really* wanted my wedding at the Cathedral Basilica." I gesture in the general direction of St. Augustine.

"And the reception at the Lightner Museum," Dorothy says in a droll tone.

"And your honeymoon at the Casa Monica Hotel," Jolene echoes, in an eerily similar tone.

I sigh contentedly. "It was the wedding of my dreams."

Jolene gently elbows Dorothy. "She's so sweet it's going to give us diabetes."

"That's not how you get it," Dorothy says and launches into a lecture about all the greens she's been unable to convince Jolene to consume.

"Where is the birthday boy?" Jolene demands, cutting short Dorothy's diatribe about kale.

I point toward the ocean. "He and Evan went surfing."

The two have become thick as thieves, and sometimes I catch myself wondering if Reagan prefers Evan to me—and I don't resent it. Not at all. Not even when they reject my offer to play Scrabble in favor of a violent video game. Nor when they have a nerf gun fight without me —all because I once said, "If you keep at this, someone might lose an eye."

"Is the party a surprise?" Jolene asks.

I nod. "Everyone's waiting. We should hurry and join them."

We head for the mansion—and yes, that is the most accurate word to describe our house.

"It's so big." Dorothy gapes at our not-so-humble abode.

"That's what she said," Jolene loudly whispers. "The first time she saw Toto, that is."

"You promised not to talk about dildos today," Dorothy hisses, flushing.

"Can I talk about real dicks?" Jolene gestures at the mansion. "More specifically, is Evan compensating for something?"

It's my turn to blush. "Our house is actually quite proportional to what you are insinuating."

"Oh." Jolene tips an invisible hat. "Is that why it's so big?"

"It was actually Reagan's idea." I narrow my eyes at Jolene so she knows any jokes about my son are off limits.

"It was?" Dorothy asks.

"He read about Florida's Homestead Exemption somewhere," I say with a grin. "And then convinced Evan that a primary residence in this state might well be worth a ton of money since no creditor can ever take it from you, not even the IRS."

"We're talking about the same Reagan who's turning ten today?" Dorothy asks.

I attempt to nod nonchalantly—a fail because I'm beaming with enough pride to start a parade.

When we reach the ornate doors, they detect the Glorp on my wrist and open automatically—an Octothorpe technology synergy that is as creepy as it is useful.

My dear Precious, do not think for a second that this door mechanism can ever adore you with the same ardor as I. It doesn't have a shrine where it worships you as a fertility goddess. It doesn't starve for the mouthwatering flakes of dead skin that you free each time you exfoliate in the shower.

When my friends walk inside, they both whistle.

Yeah. At my son's urging, Evan decided to embrace being a billionaire, so he hired a team of artists to make the lobby look like the inside of a wave—which I believe took enough crystal to run Swarovski for a year. Oh, and it doubles as a ballroom.

"Is this the whole town?" Dorothy asks in a loud whisper, eyeing the crowd camped out in said ballroom.

I grab a champagne flute from the nearest waiter. "It's just the people we know." We just happen to know this many. "The staff from the camp are here too, and so are the children." I gesture at the louder section of the ballroom. "The only people we know that we didn't invite are the annoying members of the HOA." This snub was Evan's idea of revenge because he thinks the nosy busybodies are dying to see the inside of this mansion—the biggest house in Palm Islet.

"Oh, my God." Dorothy points at the guy who is usually Evan's video-call drinking buddy but happens to be here in the flesh today.

Jolene fans herself. "The god being Thor, right? That's who that dude reminds me of."

"You don't get it," Dorothy says in wide-eyed wonder. "That's Mason Tugev."

I blink at her. "How do you know his name?"

"Doesn't everyone?" Dorothy exclaims. "He's a famous hockey player!"

Huh. Evan's never mentioned that. I could see it, though. Mason is as big as a Newfoundland, but sinewy and muscular like a pit bull, with the cold eyes of a wolf.

"Now, be honest." Jolene turns to Dorothy. "Do you really feel nothing when you look at a guy like that? No tingles whatsoever? I promise not to get jealous."

Dorothy rolls her eyes. "Give up on that already."

"Come," I say, eager to nip this conversation in the bud, in case Mason has good hearing. "Let me introduce you to my boss."

I lead them over to Calvin, explaining that as of my recent graduation, I'm officially the emergency vet at the local clinic on Tuesdays and Wednesdays.

"Why just two days?" Dorothy asks.

I point back at the door. "Our farm animals need a vet on a regular basis, and I'm it."

"Speaking of..." Calvin tugs nervously at his mustache. "Has Carrie been crying again?"

"No. The eyedrops helped." Cows don't cry to express sadness—at least as far as scientists think—but their eyes water when dry or infected, both problems solved by the drops.

"What about Charlotte?" Calvin asks. "Is her appetite better?"

"Much," I say. "Both hers and Miranda's."

"What about Samantha?" he says. "Is she—"

"Look, Calvin, all your girls are doing just fine."

Noticing my friends looking at us askance, I explain, "Calvin's pet cows now live here with us, on the farm."

"But I visit them every chance I get," Calvin says defensively.

It's true. He might visit a little too much. He also takes them to walk on the nearby beach every chance he gets.

"And I had no other choice," he continues. "The HOA gave me an ultimatum."

I'm actually shocked he was able to live in a private community and keep cows as pets for as long as he did. Nor do I understand how he handled the logistics of the cows without a farm. Even with a farm, Harry has to herd the bovines away from mischief all the time.

"Our farm is a better home for them," I tell Calvin reassuringly. "Where else can they play with a cat?"

Yep. It's a thing. Sally likes cows, and the cows like

her back despite the fact that she eats the beef version of Fancy Feast.

My phone dings with a text from Evan:

We're almost home.

"All right, everyone!" I shout. "This is a surprise party, so hide as best as you can and get ready to yell, 'Surprise!'"

Everyone does as I say, and the room grows surprisingly quiet.

The doors open, and Evan is the first to walk in.

I suck in a breath. Even after being with him for three years and receiving about 1,357 orgasms, the sight of him still makes my panties damp.

Reagan steps in next, and it could be my imagination, but I think he grew another inch in the few hours he was away. As luck would have it, his surfboard blocks his view, so I shout, "Now!"

"Surprise!" we all scream at the top of our lungs.

The yelling works a bit too well. Reagan is so startled that he accidentally smacks Boone on the head with the surfboard. Like something out of *The Three Stooges* routine, Boone waves his arms to regain his balance—and accomplishes it by grabbing one of Bonnie's ample breasts, at which point she screams like a heretic in the hands of the Inquisition.

Balance regained—but not his dignity—Boone releases the boob, and Bonnie goes silent and beet red.

"Surprise?" everyone yells at Reagan weakly.

My son drops the errant surfboard at his feet and unleashes one of his weaponized boyish grins.

Everyone relaxes, and chaos reigns for the next few minutes as our guests congratulate him and shower him with gifts. Meanwhile, Evan makes his way to me and gives me a kiss that tastes like ocean, sunshine, and orgasms.

"Ready to unveil our big surprise?" he murmurs after pulling away.

All I really want is to chase Evan to our bedroom, but maternal duty comes first, so I nod.

Taking out his phone, Evan uses an Octothorpe app to wake the giant movie-theater-sized screen on the far wall, and the first picture in the slideshow we created appears. One that simply says, "And now for the gifts from Mom and Dad."

Yep. For two years now, Reagan has been referring to Evan as Dad, and to this day, something melts in my chest every time I hear it. On some occasions, he also calls him Mr. Dad.

"Can I get everyone's attention?" Evan says loudly.

Everybody quiets down.

I catch Reagan's gaze. "Ready to see the first gift?"

"Yes!" Reagan's eyes gleam.

I suspect he knows what it is because he's been hinting very strongly at it for a few months now.

Evan shows the first slide, and lo-and-behold, it's a picture of a jet ski.

Reagan squeals in glee and tackle-hugs Evan—because he's probably guessed correctly that it was Evan who convinced me to allow my son this exorbitant and dangerous-seeming gift.

Evan actually bought three jet skis, so we can ride them together. We also agreed that Reagan will only go out on the jet ski with an adult, preferably one as good at swimming as Evan is (as opposed to myself who has a history of almost drowning).

When Reagan's excitement dies down a little, he asks, "What's the second gift?"

Ah. Right. "Remember all the times you've asked for a sister?" I ask with a smile.

It was always specifically a sister because—and I quote: "This way, I can protect her. Also, when she grows up, I can date one of her friends."

At the word "sister," my son's eyes light up even brighter. Oh, and not surprisingly, all the attendees dart glances at my stomach, followed by disapproving looks at the champagne that I'm sipping.

"Meet Ariel," I say and nod at Evan, who presses the button again, unleashing a new slideshow featuring the adorable three-year-old we've decided to foster with the goal of adoption.

Reagan watches the slideshow in excited fascination, and when it's done, he demands to know when Ariel will be joining us.

"In a few days," I say. "Our lawyers are wrapping up all the paperwork as we speak."

"I can't wait!" Reagan bounces up and down, and I know exactly how he feels. Evan and I can't wait to meet our new daughter either.

We haven't slept a wink since we learned that this is finally happening.

Reagan, being a ten-year-old, is already moving on to the next most exciting topic. "When can I ride the jet ski?" he asks, not pausing in his bounce.

"First thing tomorrow," Evan and I say in unison. We knew this question was coming so we came prepared.

"Cool." Reagan gestures toward the boisterous noise. "I'm going to go say hi to my friends."

He dashes away to where the camp kids are, and Evan and I grin at each other, then go mingle with the rest of the guests. My heart isn't in it, though. I want to watch Reagan be happy—but he's now of that age where I'd embarrass him if I got too close when he's with friends. Also, a part of me wants to fast-forward through the next few days until Ariel is here. Or at the very least, I'd like to fast-forward through this party so I can be alone with Evan in our ginormous bedroom.

Alas, the party is just beginning.

"When did you decide to adopt?" Jolene asks when we get to her and Dorothy.

"Six months ago," Evan replies, wrapping his arm around my shoulders.

"Sorry I didn't tell you guys," I say sheepishly. "I didn't want to jinx anything."

"I'm just surprised," Dorothy says. "All you've talked about lately is IVF."

Evan and I exchange a glance, and he nods, confirming that he's okay with me sharing this with my closest friends.

"We've done that too," I say. "And we now have a

frozen embryo—a boy—for when we want to grow our family further."

"Wow," Dorothy says.

"Tell me all about it," Jolene says. "Don't leave out a single detail."

I know she's asking about IVF because she's been thinking about something that sounds equally like a neat idea and something from a Jerry Springer episode: using Dorothy's egg and Jolene's brother's sperm to make a baby that Jolene would carry to term.

Evan—who doesn't know any of this—tells them about our journey, and I join in from time to time. After that, we go mingle with more people and drink more champagne.

The champagne makes me extra aware of how sexy Evan is, and when the dancing starts, I'm just about ready to jump his bones. After what feels like a year of forced celibacy, folks finally start to leave—or head to the guest rooms upstairs in the case of the out-of-state visitors. A few more chaste hours later, Evan and I finally find ourselves alone—and a little tipsy, at least on my end.

"Race you there," I say with a grin and sprint for the bedroom.

Evan is either even more drunk than I am, or he lets me win—no doubt because he likes the way my bosom heaves after a sprint.

"That was a great party." Eyes heated, Evan locks the door and puts on some sexy music.

"It was." I let my cocktail dress drop to the floor. "Amazing."

Evan strips just as swiftly, unleashing Vitamin D in all its splendor. "Take those panties off," he demands.

I do as I'm told, then preemptively slip off my bra and let my hair down.

"Just like that. Now bend over the bed." Evan accompanies his order with a stroke of his cock.

I get into the position he wants me in, and then I flush as I feel the cool AC air on the soaking-wet parts of me. The skin on my legs breaks out in gooseflesh.

"Touch yourself." Evan's voice is right behind me, his warm breath on my bottom.

Biting my cheek, I press on my clit just as Evan's tongue slides between my butt cheeks.

Oh, wow.

It starts to move.

Double wow.

I moan as a monster of an orgasm coils in my core.

Evan's tongue performs more ministrations.

I'm getting closer.

The ministrations slow, making me groan pleadingly.

"I want you inside," I pant, clutching the sheets.

Evan pulls his tongue away. "Inside where?"

"You know where."

"You have to say it."

"My ass." Despite asking for this about two hundred times, my cheeks—on my face and lower—turn crimson. "Please, Evan."

He grunts approvingly. "I like it when you beg."

With that, he pours some silky lubricant on the spot where his tongue was a moment ago and enters me with a finger.

Oh, God, yeah.

Two fingers.

Oh, that's good. Full, almost uncomfortable, but oh-so good.

With desperation, I rub my clit as the very tip of Vitamin D replaces Evan's fingers and moves in deeper, filling me, stretching me almost to the point of pain but never quite getting there. Instead, the sensation is textured, layered, the growing tension inside me so powerful I have to pant through it.

He pushes in deeper, and my nerve endings explode, the pleasure streaking down my spine and making me shudder all over, clenching around his invading cock.

Evan groans. "Oh, yeah. That's a good start." His callused fingers replace mine on my clit as he slowly pushes deeper still. "Now I want you to come together with me."

All I can do is gasp out his name, then scream it as his fingers work me over.

"That's it." Evan penetrates my pussy with a finger, and the double stretch is the last straw my orgasm needed.

With an incoherent cry, I come, my ass squeezing his cock so hard he grunts, "Oh, fuck!" and then I feel the warm jets of his release deep inside me.

We collapse onto the bed together, and it takes several

minutes before we find the strength to drag ourselves to the bathroom and clean up.

"That wasn't *exactly* us coming together," I grumble once I'm back in bed and cradled in his arms. "More like falling dominoes."

He kisses my nape. "That just means we need a little bit more practice."

I grin contentedly. I know I will enjoy said practice, just as I enjoy anything and everything that has to do with this man.

With Evan, my life is a vacation that will never end.

Sneak Peeks

Thank you for participating in Brooklyn and Evan's journey!

Ready for more hot billionaires? Check out *Billionaire Grump*, a fake relationship romcom about a sharp-tongued aspiring botanist, a sexy, Ancient Rome-obsessed grump, and one fateful encounter in an elevator that goes hilariously wrong.

Love single parent romances? Read *Billionaire Rake*! Adrian Westfield has it all: money, looks, and a beautiful daughter. But when he's forced into a custody battle with his toxic ex, there's one more thing he desperately needs: a fake wife.

To make sure you never miss a release, sign up for the newsletter at mishabell.com.

Turn the page to read previews from *Billionaire Grump* and *Billionaire Rake*!

Excerpt from Billionaire Grump
BY MISHA BELL

Juno

When I'm late for a job interview and get stuck on an elevator with an annoyingly sexy, Ancient Rome-obsessed grump, the last thing I expect is for him to be the billionaire owner of the building. I also don't expect to almost kill him... accidentally, of course.

Sure, I don't get the plant care position I applied for, but I do receive an interesting offer.

Lucius needs to trick the public (and his grandma) into thinking he's in a relationship, and I need tuition money to get my botany degree. Our arrangement is mutually beneficial—that is, until I start catching feelings.

If being a cactus lover has taught me anything, it's that if you get too close, there's a good chance you'll end up hurt.

Lucius

Post-elevator incident, I'm left with three things: my favorite water bottle full of pee, a life threatening allergic reaction, and paparazzi photos of my "girl-friend" and I that make my Gram the happiest woman alive.

Naturally, my next step is to blackmail—I mean, convince—this (admittedly cute) girl to pretend to date me. That way, my grandma stays happy, and as a bonus, I can keep the gold diggers at bay.

Unfortunately, my arch nemesis, a.k.a. biology, kicks in, and the whole "not getting physical" part of our agreement becomes increasingly hard to abide by. Worse yet, the longer I'm with Juno, the more my delicately crafted icy exterior melts away.

If I'm not careful, Juno will tear down my walls completely.

———

"Are you calling me stupid?" I snap. Anyone could have trouble with these damn buttons, not just a person with dyslexia.

He looks pointedly at the buttons. "Stupid is as stupid does."

I grind my teeth, painfully. "You're an asshole. And you've watched *Forrest Gump* one too many times."

His lips flatten. "That movie wasn't the origin of that saying. It's from Latin: *Stultus est sicut stultus facit.*"

I roll my eyes. "What kind of pretentious *stultus* quotes Latin?"

The steel in his eyes is so cold I bet my tongue would get stuck if I tried to lick his eyeball. "I don't know. Maybe the 'idiot' who happens to like everything related to Rome, including their numerals."

My jaw drops open. "You made this decision?" I wave toward the elevator buttons.

He nods.

Shit. He probably heard me earlier, which means I started the insults. In my defense, he did make an idiotic choice.

I exhale a frustrated breath. "If you're such an expert on Roman numerals, you could've told me which one to press."

He crosses his arms over his chest. "You didn't ask me."

My hackles rise again. "Ask you? You looked like you might bite my head off for just existing."

"That's because you delayed—"

The elevator jerks to a stop, and the lights around us dim.

We both stare at the doors.

They stay shut.

He turns to me and narrows his eyes accusingly. "What did you press now?"

"Me? How? I've been facing you. Unfortunately."

With an annoying headshake, he stalks toward the

panel with the buttons, and I have to leap away before I get trampled.

"You probably pressed something earlier," he mutters. "Why else would we be stuck?"

Why is it illegal to choke people? Just a few seconds with my hands on his throat would be a calming exercise.

Instead, I glare at his back, which is blocking my view of what he's doing, if anything. "The poor elevator probably just committed suicide over these Roman numerals. It knew that when someone sees things like L and XL, they think of T-shirt sizes for Neanderthal types like you. And don't get me started on that XXX button, which is a clear reference to porn. It creates a hostile work env—"

"Can you shut up so I can get us out of this?" he snaps.

His words bring home the reality of our situation: it's been over a minute, and the doors are still closed.

Dear saguaro, am I really stuck here? With this guy? What about my interview?

"Silence, finally," he says with satisfaction and moves to the side, so I see him jam his finger at the "help" button.

"It's a miracle that's not in Latin," I can't help but say. "Or Klingon."

"Hello?" he says into the speaker under the button, his voice dripping with irritation.

No reply, not even static.

"Anyone there?" His annoyance is clearly rising to new heights. "I'm late for an important meeting."

"And I'm late for an interview," I chime in, in case it matters.

He pauses to arch a thick eyebrow at me. "An interview? For what position?"

I stand straighter. "I'm sure the likes of you don't realize this, but the plants in this building don't take care of themselves."

Wait. Have I said too much? Could he torpedo my interview—assuming this elevator snafu hasn't done it already? What does he do here, anyway—design ridiculous elevators? That can't be a full-time job, can it?

"A tree hugger," he mutters under his breath. "That tracks."

What an asshole. I've never hugged a tree in my life. I'm too busy talking to them.

He returns his scowling attention to the "help" button—though now I'm thinking it should've been labeled as "no help."

"Hello? Can you hear me?" he shouts. "Answer now, or you're fired."

I roll my eyes. "Is it a good idea to be a dick to the person who can save us?"

He blows out an audible breath. "It doesn't matter. The button must be malfunctioning. They wouldn't dare ignore me."

I pull out my trusty phone, a nice and simple Nokia 3310. "Full of yourself much?"

He stares at my hands incredulously. "So that's why the elevator got stuck. It went through a time warp and transported us to 2008."

I frown at the lack of reception on my Nokia. "This version was released in 2017."

"It still looks dumber than a brain-dead crash test dummy." He proudly pulls an iPhone from his pocket. "*This* is what a phone should look like."

I scoff. "That's what constant distraction looks like. Anyway, if your iNotSoSmartPhone—trademarked—is so great, it should have some reception, right?"

He glances at his screen, but I can tell he already knows the truth: no reception for his darling either.

Still, I can't resist. "See? Your genius of a phone is just as useless. All it's good for is turning people into social-media-checking zombies."

He hides the device, like a protective parent. "On top of all your endearing qualities, you're a technophobe too?"

I debate throwing my Nokia at his head but decide it's not worth shelling out sixty-five bucks for a replacement. "Just because I don't want to be distracted doesn't mean I'm a technophobe."

"Actually, my phone is great at blocking out distractions." He puts the headphones back over his ears. "See?" He presses play, and I hear the faint riffs of heavy metal.

"Very mature," I mouth at him.

"Sorry," he says overly loudly. "I can't hear any distractions."

Fine. Whatever. At least he has good taste in music. My cactus and I are big fans of Metallica, which is what I think he's listening to.

I begin to pace back and forth.

I'm stuck, and I'm late. If this elevator jam doesn't resolve itself in the next minute or two, I can pretty much kiss the new job goodbye—and by extension, my tuition money. No tuition money means no botany degree, which has been my dream for the last few years.

By saguaro's juices, this sucks really bad.

I sneak a glance at the hottie—I mean, asshole.

What would he say about someone with dyslexia wanting a college degree? Probably that I'd need a university that uses coloring books. In truth, even coloring books wouldn't help that much—I can never stay inside those stupid lines.

I sigh and look away, increasingly worried. My dreams aside, what if the elevator stays stuck for a while?

The most immediate problem is my growing need to pee—but paradoxically, a longer-term worry will be finding liquids to drink.

I wonder... If you're thirsty enough, does your body reabsorb the water from the bladder? Also, could I MacGyver a filter to reclaim the water in my urine with what I have on me? Maybe through cat hair?

I shiver, and only partially from the insane AC that's somehow reaching me even in here. In the short term, it would be so much better if it were hot instead of cold. I'd sweat out the liquids and not need to pee, though I guess I'd die of thirst sooner. I sneak an envious glance at the large stranger. I bet he has a bladder the size of a blimp. He also has a stainless-steel bottle that's probably filled with water that he likely won't share.

There's also the question of food. I don't have

anything edible with me, apart from a can of cat food... and, theoretically, the cat herself.

No. I'd sooner eat this stranger than poor Atonic.

As if psychic, the stranger's stomach growls.

Crap. With this guy being so big and mean, he'd probably eat the cat. After that, he'd eat me... and not in a fun way.

I'm so, so screwed.

————

Visit www.mishabell.com to order your copy of *Billionaire Grump* today!

Excerpt from Billionaire Rake

BY MISHA BELL

He's a billionaire... and a rake.

Yes, I know it's not the 1800s. I'm just a bit obsessed with historical romance, that's all. And books in general, which is why I'm on my way to interview for my dream job at the library when Adrian Westfield's sheep-like hound knocks me over and into the mud. So I'm late, dirty, and completely flub my interview—only to get the offer of my life.

To win custody of his baby daughter, Adrian Westfield wants to make me his fake wife.

———

"Why not wait at the library?" Mom asks, and though we're talking on the phone, I can sense the worry on her kind face. "I thought this interview was important."

Important is an understatement. This librarian job is The One Ring, and I'm Gollum for it.

Gripping the phone tighter, I look around at my picturesque Central Park surroundings. "I knew sitting in the waiting room for too long would make me nervous, so I took a promenade." Not that it helped much.

Mom gasps audibly. "Is 'promenade' what the kids are calling Xanax these days?"

I almost drop my phone into the serene waters of the nearby lake. "A promenade is a leisurely walk in a public place. Sorry—another one of those historical romance words."

"Oh." Mom sounds way too relieved, considering I've never done drugs. "Make sure to tell them how much you like those books."

Huh. Saying that I merely *like* historical romance is like saying Glenn Close's character was kind of into Michael Douglas in *Fatal Attraction*. Or that Hannibal Lecter was peckish for human livers with fava beans in *The Silence of the Lambs*.

The alarm on my phone goes off, spiking my heartbeat. "It's time to head over there," I tell Mom. "I only have ten minutes before my interview starts, and it's a five-minute walk."

"Go then," Mom says. "Hurry. I'm sure you'll crush it."

"Thanks." Hanging up, I smooth the skirt of the suit I bought with the last of my money—clothes I'll have to return if I don't get the job.

But I will, of course. This library has the best collection of historical romance in the world, and I'm the most avid historical romance reader there is. It's a match made in Victorian England.

Miss Miller tightens her stifling corset, readjusts her bonnet, and lifts her chin. During trying times such as this, a lady must keep a stiff upper lip.

Yes, that's better. When I need to calm down or cheer myself up, I often cast myself in the role of a nineteenth-century lady named Miss Jane Miller. She's the daughter of a baron who impregnated her mother out of wedlock and then promptly died on a ship that was hunting sperm whales. According to survivors, the good baron was humped to death by the majestic beast's eight-foot cock—which, to me, seems like a fittingly ironic fate for a useless sperm donor.

To further relax myself, I pop in my headphones and play the theme from Netflix's *Bridgerton*.

A menacing white shadow appears in the corner of my eye.

I turn, and my already-pounding heart nearly jumps out of my throat as I freeze on the spot, a dozen questions forming in my mind.

Is that a sheep? If so, what's it doing in Manhattan? Why is it running at me? Is it wagging its tail? Can you be killed by a—

Snapping out of my stupor, I attempt to move out of the ruminant's path, but it's too late. The massive thing is already upon me, standing on its hind devil-hooves and

plopping its front ones on my shoulders with the force of
Thor's hammer.

I fly backward.

The ground slams into me.

Air rushes out of my lungs, and it's a struggle to
breathe.

There's thick liquid all around me.

Blood? Brains?

No, worse.

It's mud. Mud that probably saved me from an
injury but has destroyed my hopes of looking
presentable.

I suck in some air and thank God I'm not dead. As
far as embarrassing ways to die go, getting killed by a
sheep is up there with getting mauled by a hamster and
licked to death by a kitten. The fact that I'd die a twenty-
three-year-old virgin would just be the cherry on top of a
multilayered shit-cake.

The sheep is right in my face now. Is it about to eat
my eyelids? Or chew the glasses that, by some miracle, are
still on my nose?

Nope. It licks my cheek.

Its breath smells like chicken and sweet potatoes.

What the hell?

Wait a second. This sheep's fur smells suspiciously
like a wet dog. Almost as if—

"I'm so sorry," says the sheep in a deep, rich, smooth-
as-melted-chocolate voice. "The leash slipped from my
hands."

"You're a dog?" I ask the sheep, my mind still muddled.

"I'm not," it—or whoever—says. "I'm Adrian. The dog is Leo, and he sounds like this." The voice changes to sound an octave higher and sped up, like this person has eaten an overcaffeinated chipmunk. "You smell good. The mud is fun. I'm sorry I made you fall. Sometimes I forget I'm not a puppy anymore."

The dog that is not a sheep—Leo—moves out of my view, and I finally spot the speaker.

The sight evaporates whatever air I've reclaimed.

The man's—Adrian's—face is perfectly proportioned, with an aristocratic nose, a powerful chin, and silver-colored eyes that gleam roguishly. Yes, roguishly. With his broad shoulders and dark, windswept hair that extends past his ears, he could be copy-pasted onto a historical romance book cover; all they'd need to do is Photoshop in some period clothing.

Taken by the Duke, the title of said romance would read. Or *Marquess's Reluctant Bride. Thy Name is Earl. Baron's Virgin Mistress. Scoundrel Viscount's Wallflower*—

He kneels next to me.

Are my glasses fogging up, or my retinas? Such unadulterated handsomeness should come with a warning.

"Are you okay?" he asks.

Am I? I'm anxious, shaken, and much too turned on considering my predicament, but mostly, I feel like I'm forgetting something extremely important.

Then it hits me.

The interview! How could I forget about that, even for a moment? Do I have windmills in my head?

"I'm late," I announce and move to sit up.

Hell's bells. My arms flail, and chunks of mud fly in every direction—including toward Leo, who licks them eagerly, and Adrian, who takes it stoically.

"Are you sure you're ready to get up?" Adrian asks as he extends his hand to me.

"It doesn't matter if I'm ready." I grab his hand—and then nearly collapse back on the ground in a fit of the vapors.

His skin is hot like a raging furnace, and that heat permeates my body, melting everything in its wake.

Uh-oh. Miss Miller feels a yearning in her most secret place. A most unladylike tingle that—

"I don't think you've recovered yet," Adrian says as he helps me get to my feet. "Let's have you sit on that bench over there."

"Can't," I pant, pulling my hand out of his grasp before I combust. "Must run."

His expression hardens. "You could have a concussion."

"And whose fault is that?" I narrow my eyes at him. "I'm late for an interview. For my dream job. Can you stop getting in my way?"

"An interview?" He drags his gaze over me. "Looking like that?"

I glance down and wish I hadn't. "Oh, no. I'm dirtier than a pig."

"Pigs aren't actually dirty," Adrian says. "They use mud to cool off, and as sunscreen and bug repellent."

Miss Miller fights the urge to slap the scoundrel's high-cheekboned face.

"That's such a helpful lesson in husbandry, thanks." I step out of the mud. My knees are wobbly at first, but with each step, I'm feeling more and more like myself—just a much, much filthier version.

"Wait," he calls after me. "Let me at least help you."

I don't wait, but he catches up with me and grabs my elbow—like we're about to go for a stroll before teatime.

Once again, my treacherous body reacts to his touch with the most inappropriate intensity.

Sheesh. If by some miracle I get this job, I'll have to move Project Grand Deflowering to the top of my to-do list. Not getting any for so long has clearly turned me into a hormonal powder keg, ready to blow the first stranger I meet.

Miss Miller finds that last thought unseemly.

"Would they let you reschedule?" Adrian asks, still keeping a hold of my elbow.

"I doubt it," I say. "I wouldn't."

"It's just that I live right across the street," he says. "We could get your clothes laundered in an hour."

I blush like the maiden I am. "Are you trying to get me out of my clothes?"

His smile is cocky. "Do. Or do not. There is no try."

I free my arm from his. "Keep Yoda in your pants."

A total rake. I should've figured.

Speeding up, I leave him behind—for a second, anyway.

"Hold on." He catches up with me, Leo panting at his heels. "I meant the laundry offer."

"And *I* mean this: even if I weren't in a rush, the answer would be 'hell no.'"

He sighs. "Can I at least—"

"This is my destination," I say breathlessly as I halt next to the library. "It was not a pleasure meeting you."

He smiles wickedly. "The lack of pleasure was all mine."

———

Visit www.mishabell.com to order your copy of *Billionaire Rake* today!

Made in United States
North Haven, CT
02 March 2024

49353341R00163